ONE
CHOICE
AWAY

Book Two: Symphony's story continued...

A Novel by

Natasha Simmons

One Choice Away

ISBN-13: 978-0-9967127-4-3
ISBN-10: 0-9967127-4-7

Published by Thomas Publishing

One Choice Away

To Phil, with love. See…I listen.

N.S.

ACKNOWLEDGMENTS

Thank you to my daughters, Kori and Kendall, who were harassed incessantly to read lines, paragraphs, pages, and tell me quickly what they thought. To my son, Dorian, who cooked and ran errands when I was "in the zone" of writing. I appreciate my book club Divas for "gently" encouraging me to finish Symphony's story. And to all my readers who patiently waited for the rest of Symphony's story, I'm eternally grateful for your continued support.

A special thanks to Jessica. Your comments throughout the edits were uplifting. Bobbie Thurman, thank you for your extra pair of eyes on my manuscript. Thank you, Traci Tucker, for allowing me to take up a corner of your bar for hours at a time, while I pecked out this story. I am eternally grateful to have a friend who owns a winery. Writing and wine are a must. I also appreciate you reading through the manuscript to make sure everything was just right. Your support and encouragement means more than you'll ever know.

One Choice Away

We are one choice away from changing our lives…

Symphony

Symphony James refused to listen to the quiet invitations fear whispered to her. They coaxed her, begged her, almost forced her to embrace a reality she almost couldn't help herself from believing. She knew what faced her. Yes, she was afraid, but giving in to that fear would only add to her anxiety, and the doctor said she had to stay relaxed.

For the past two months, she'd been propped up in bed, just barely allowed to walk to the toilet on her own. Despite the bed rest and being away from Florida, Symphony thoroughly enjoyed bonding with her new friend Alexandra Wyatt Phoenix at her Baton Rouge home, as well as creating a special friendship with the housekeeper Carla Faye Briggs. Carla Faye fussed over her like a mother hen—it was annoying and comforting all at once.

At first, Symphony refused Alex's offer to stay at her childhood home, but necessity forced Symphony to strip away the pride that made her think she could do everything on her own. Symphony quickly realized staying hidden away in Baton Rouge was the perfect solution.

After allowing herself to fall in love *again* and realizing she'd made a mistake *again*, she needed to disappear. Especially since she was pregnant.

Symphony knew she needed to tell Kyle he was going to be a father. It didn't matter how she felt about him; she knew she would not deny her daughter nor Kyle the right to each other. She stared at the papers on the nightstand. Alex had prepared them for her—just in case.

Tears stung her eyes.

Just in case was a strong possibility.

"No!...I don't understand…Look, Jackson, I just want it to be over. Do whatever you have to do. I know I should've taken care of this long ago…No, I didn't know she was still in New Orleans. And I definitely didn't know she was damn near living on the streets!"

Kyle slammed his hand against the brick wall of his studio. Pain shot through his palm but was buried by his frustration in trying to wrap his mind around seeing Shelia again, and seeing her so thrown away. Hadn't he given her the means to do better?

"I don't give a damn about the extra costs! I'll fly to Mars if that's what it takes!" With the cell phone pressed to his ear, he dragged the other hand roughly back and forth across his forehead. "Ok…ok. Yes, I got it… I said, I got it!" He clicked off the phone and squeezed it with a shaking fist, trying to keep from flinging it into the wall.

Five months.

It had been five whole months.

He'd spent every second since Symphony walked out on him five months ago in New Orleans searching, thinking, and wondering how to get her back. He was no closer to an answer now than he'd been then.

He didn't get an opportunity to explain why he'd married Shelia, or why he felt like he'd owed her for saving his life.

He'd married her to save her life in return.

Kyle closed his eyes, but the throbbing in his head only seemed to get louder and more intense. He sat at his desk, and the bills staring back at him only intensified his anxiety and anger. He pushed the envelopes away. He hadn't been able to make any extra money with his golf lessons because he was always on the go, looking for Symphony.

His only hope to pay the lawyer and other legal fees, which included the exorbitant amount Shelia demanded for her *neglect and suffering*, was to sell the studio or go back into the depths of hell, which he didn't feel he was strong enough to do. He'd been happy to serve his country in the Army, but his tours of duty had left him emotionally battered. Kyle did not want to go back to any kind of war. But if he didn't, the only other option was to sell the shop.

How in the world could he do that?

His dad worked hard to establish their photography studio while he was growing up. It technically belonged to him now, but in his heart, it

would always be his dad's business. And if he lost it…
Not *if—when* he lost it because he saw no other
reasonable way, he would forever feel like a failure.

One stupid decision was going to change his
life forever. What was Shelia thinking? How could she
do this to him? He'd had to talk her into marrying him
because it was the only way she could get the
treatments she needed.

He'd owed her after all that shit from high
school, but this was not part of the deal. This was not
the Shelia he knew.

A long-frustrated growl climbed its way out of
his throat.

No!
No!
No!

Kyle covered his face with his hands, hating the
defeat and hopelessness that slowly squeezed his
throat.

He couldn't lose the studio. He would not let
that happen. There was no other way but to take the
freelance job Jigsaw offered him. His real name was
Jacob Lawrence, but everyone called him Jigsaw, or
Jig. He didn't know why, but the name fit the reckless
man, who never seemed to get enough adventure.

Jig was known for taking on nearly impossible projects because he was disgustingly rich, bored, and more than a tad bit reckless at times. Currently he was working on a project for a documentary.

A few weeks ago, Jigsaw asked Kyle to join him on an adventure to capture on film the exodus, displacement, and struggles of different groups of refugees. He wanted a two-month commitment, but the job would pay enough to secure Kyle's future. Which, in turn, included securing a chance with Symphony. During that time, he would not be able to search for Symphony or be available if she decided to return any of the hundreds of messages he'd left at her bakery or on her cell. Communication would be nearly impossible while he was gone

Kyle was at the end of his rope. He knew if he had to crawl through the underbelly of hell for the next two months to get rid of Shelia and keep himself financially viable, then he was damn well going to do it.

Symphony had given him air when they met less than a year ago. And then she just disappeared. His life was shit without her. All he knew was that she'd fallen completely off the grid and that Ian was running her bakery.

He'd traveled twice to South Carolina, to the home her aunt left her, with no luck. And Alexandra Phoenix refused to tell him Symphony's whereabouts.

In two months, he would have the means to ramp up his search, but when he did, he didn't want to be married to another person or be homeless. So, he picked up the phone.

"Jig. It's Kyle…when do we leave?"

Chapter One

Two months later…

"It really doesn't matter what happened between the two of you. It's irrelevant," Alexandra said.

He watched her walk around the large desk that still wore the presence of her dad in every carved detail. He could feel it, even though he'd never met the man.

"It appears to me that if you would've shown up years ago, there would be no need for this frantic search that, from what I've heard from Josh and Landon, is keeping you from the business at Phoenix Industries."

"Business is the farthest thing from my mind, right now. I don't have time to worry about contracts and acquisitions." He paused. "Plus, I've taken care of everything at work." Terry fell into the chair across from her.

"Maybe you should make more time," she said, her eyes serious.

There was something in her tone that told him the shrewd lawyer wife of his cousin knew more than he did about the business deal he was working on *and* using it to be evasive about the woman he'd been desperately seeking for the past seven months.

He pierced a glare at her, and for the first time since she'd married into his family, he saw her flinch. It burned away so quickly, maybe he'd imagined it— but no. He was certain he hadn't. Alexandra Wyatt Phoenix was hiding something.

Terry Phoenix had arrived at Alex's Baton Rouge home only twenty minutes before. For seven months, he'd been up and down the coast searching for Symphony James, the woman he was determined to never let go again—if he could find her. He was sure Alex knew the whereabouts of her new friend.

Symphony had disappeared like a ghost on the edges of a dream. He was determined to tell her he'd made a mistake all those years ago when he allowed her to call things off between the two of them.

Terry knew he'd neglected his work in the meantime, but he didn't think his current deal was lacking too much of his attention. Or was it?

He sat up straighter.

Craig and Yu Consolidations was in the bag.

At least that's what he thought, according to the documents his office manager, Leslie, messaged over to him yesterday evening before he left Boston. Could there be something wrong? Had he missed anything? This was supposed to be the deal that got him from under the shadow of his cousins. Ethan had entrusted this deal to him even though Terry was still a babe in the business.

"What do you want, Terry?"

He looked across the desk at Alex. She was sitting in the huge leather chair. It somehow made her look smaller than usual. For the first time, he noticed how tired she appeared. Her eyes wore dark circles that he'd never seen before.

Terry thought about the question she'd asked. *What did he want?* She knew exactly what he wanted. He wanted Symphony, and he wasn't leaving until Alex was honest with him.

Where was she?

Terry stared into Alex's eyes, and the sudden sadness waiting there startled him. He'd not expected the sense of hopelessness he saw. Alexandra sighed, almost as if she couldn't wait to share a burden she had buried inside.

"Terry, I—" The office door opened, and his cousin, Joshua, walked in carrying a mug. He placed the mug on the desk, and Alex wrapped her hands around it gratefully. Joshua looked across the desk at his cousin. He didn't seem at all surprised to see Terry sitting there. He, too, looked as if he was relieved that he was there.

"What?" Terry asked. The question was spoken low, on the verge of a tremble. He braced himself. It was bad. He could see it in their troubled eyes—in Alex's need to sit behind the desk. As if she needed to place a barrier between a hurtful truth she had to share with a person she knew would not be able to accept it.

Terry's eyes darted from Joshua to Alex. "What is it?" he asked, inhaling deeply. "Do you know where Symphony is? I want the truth."

Alex's head dipped slowly into a nod. "We'd planned on calling you today before it was too late. Everything just happened so quickly."

Chapter Two

I want the truth.
Even if it hurts?
Yes, even if it hurts.

Anyone who said they always preferred the truth over a lie was a liar.

Terry Phoenix would have fully embraced a lie with his entire being rather than have the truth digging a hole in his chest with a rusty shovel. Everything here was too much.

The harsh white fluorescent lights were too exposing.

Nothing could hide here.

Not even reality, as it was vulnerably splayed out, naked and exposed by the light.

The sounds.

They were too raw.

The constant beeps of the machines and the ragged pull and release of artificial breathing sawed through his soul.

Terry's nose burned from the antiseptic in the air, and the floor cleaner being used in the passageway nearly choked him.

The nurse let him in because there was no other family. She believed that, in these situations, love was the best doctor available. Besides, the jagged desperation on Terry's face told her that he was in pain. Only love caused that kind of pain, so she let him in to visit for the allotted fifteen minutes.

Symphony James had given the world the most precious thing she'd ever created, and she now lay hovering just outside the reaches of the arms of death for the sacrifice. Her daughter was born healthy and loud. Her mother, however, never got the chance to see or hear her.

Symphony James lay in a coma. Her blood pressure was so high when the paramedics arrived soon after Alex found her, that they were sure she'd had a stroke. By nature, Symphony went to bed early because she was used to being up and at the bakery so early in the morning. Alex had gone in to check on her when she saw her light still on in the middle of the night.

That was a week ago.

An entire week ago when the doctors performed an emergency cesarean. She was only a week early—actually scheduled to have the baby in another couple of days. The doctors still considered the baby full-term, which was surprising since she'd been on bedrest for so long. Due dates were not an exact science, and at thirty-nine weeks, the baby was born big and healthy.

For Terry, finding out about the baby felt like a punch in the gut. When he'd envisioned himself with a family, Symphony was there, along with the children they adored.

His dreams were just that now—dreams. The woman he loved was laid out before him with a machine helping her breathe, recovering from a pregnancy he had nothing to do with. The fiery halo of her hair splayed out on the pillow was the only warmth in the room.

"I'm so sorry, Symphony." He squeezed her hand, his voice paper-thin. "It's all my fault. I should never have let you walk away from me." By the time Terry had come back into her life, she was already seeing Kyle. But even then, he should have made her see that her future belonged with him and no other man.

Terry spent the next few minutes reassuring Symphony that he was there to take care of her, no matter how long it took. He talked to her in hushed tones about the times they'd shared during college, the nights they spent together in her aunt's bakery, and the plans for their future he should have shared with her long before. He also told her about his work and a few funny stories about his clients. He wasn't so certain about his current client, but he couldn't dwell on that right now.

Symphony was his top priority.

"Sir?" Terry looked up into the kind eyes of the nurse who'd let him in to see Symphony. "Time's up," she whispered quietly. "You can come back this evening. I have you listed as Ms. James's fiancé."

Terry glanced once again at Symphony, kissed her cheek lightly, ignoring the tubes and sounds of the machines, and whispered, "I'll see you in a little while, sweetheart." He stood, thanked the nurse again, and found a chair in the waiting room. There was an elderly woman with two middle-aged men clutching each of her hands, grief lining all their faces.

He took a seat away from them, to give them as much privacy as he could. He had no intention of going anywhere until Symphony was leaving the hospital with him.

Terry looked up at the muted TV but wasn't really paying attention to whatever they were talking about on CNN. He sat there, staring up at that TV for hours, it felt. He probably should've been making sure his deal wasn't caving in, but his mind was full with thoughts of Symphony. He prayed to whomever was listening that she would recover.

After the woman, and the men with her, left the waiting area, the only people who came and left were people in scrubs getting coffee from the small nook that held coffee, cups, and water.

"How is she?" Alex asked as she settled in the chair next to Terry. "Any changes?"

"I don't know. The nurse says she's stable, but I don't know what that means, and she wasn't very forthcoming with information. I guess she figured she'd breached enough of the rules just by letting me in there."

Alex placed her hand on Terry's. He slipped his hand away, stood, and paced a bit. He pushed his hands in the pockets of his jeans. From somewhere, he heard the cry of a baby and suddenly stopped pacing. He frowned and turned an expectant face to Alex.

Alex's eyes were suddenly hooded with sadness.

"The baby is gone."

Terry sucked in a quick breath as his eyes widened. Alex knew instantly what he was thinking and quickly added, "She's fine, Terry." She knew he was relieved when his eyes closed and he took a slow deep breath, bowing his head to his chest.

"The baby?... She?... A girl?" He had so many questions as he sank into the chair he'd previously vacated. Symphony had a baby girl. She was probably a miniature version of her mother—beautiful and perfect. It was the first time he'd thought about the baby since Alex told him how Symphony had ended up in the hospital. "What do you mean, she's gone?" He was shocked by the emotions that suddenly consumed him.

"Just that. Symphony is in a coma, she has no family that I'm aware of…"

"So, where's the baby?" Terry cut her off his voice rising.

Alex was taken aback by the intensity in his tone. "Uh…I…" She stuttered, which was not like her at all. She quickly recovered. "First of all," she straightened, "I'm just the damn messenger. You need to calm the hell down."

Terry saw that she was about to go into full-on feisty mode. He threw up his hands. "I'm sorry…I'm sorry, Alex. I didn't mean for it to come out as an attack. You can back down a bit." For the first time in what seemed like a very long while, they both smiled with the release of tension.

Alex shook her head. "You Phoenix men are so impatient." Her eyes clouded again. Terry's mirrored hers. "The baby…" she paused, a soft smile lighting her face again, "Cadence…the baby's name is Cadence."

"Cadence." Terry repeated, testing the sound of the name of Symphony's daughter. "Cadence James." He whispered to himself, looking away from Alex— already thinking about Cadence curiously wondering around on wobbly legs when she grew to be a toddler.

"Dean." Alex corrected him, gently.

Terry's forehead bunched when he looked back to Alex. "Huh?"

As tenderly as she could, she said, "The baby's name is Cadence Alexandra Dean." Pride showed all over Alex's face as she announced Cadence's middle name—her namesake.

Terry couldn't focus on Alex's glow of pride; he was too busy feeling the sharp punch of the baby's last name directly in his abdomen. He couldn't breathe. He was paralyzed once again by the stark reality that the woman he loved was in a coma, and she'd given birth to a baby that wasn't his.

Alex knew there was nothing she could do or say to ease Terry's pain, but she reached over the arm of the chair anyway to pull him into a hug. He crumbled in her arms and cried for the family that he felt was lost before he could ever have them.

Chapter Three

It took Terry a while to recover, but when he did become coherent enough to listen, Alex told him the baby was with her grandparents in Florida. She got up and went to the coffee pot. Alex pushed a cup of coffee on Terry, but he refused, wanting to get back to the conversation, pretty sure the coffee was stale.

"Florida?"

"Yes, that's where Kyle's parents live."

"Kyle's *parents*?"

"Yes, Symphony is estranged from her own parents, so she had papers drawn up to make sure Kyle got custody in case something went wrong."

Terry knew that Symphony had not spoken to her parents since Aunt Helen received custody of her. It was one of the reasons she had abandonment issues. And one of the reasons he felt awful about letting her walk away from him. He was sure she felt that he gave up on her just like her parents had.

"Why did she think something would go wrong?" he asked. Were there issues with her that he didn't know about?

"She was sick the entire pregnancy, and her blood pressure was often off the charts."

"Why?" Terry asked.

Alex was exhausted, and his questions were making her relive all the scary moments she'd endured with her friend. "It happens sometimes during pregnancy, Terry. She just happened to be in that small percentage of women who…well…" She didn't want to say that Symphony was in that small window of women who died from the effects of pregnancy. "…suffered more than other women."

"Why did Kyle's parents take the baby away from its mother?" A thought suddenly occurred to him, and he wondered why it hadn't hit him sooner. "Where is Kyle? Why isn't he here? Why doesn't he have his daughter?"

His daughter.

Symphony's baby is *Kyle's* daughter too.

He looked around the waiting room as if mentioning his name would make the man appear. His sole focus had been on Symphony that he hadn't given Kyle a second thought until he heard the baby's last name, but Terry's anguish had pushed the man out of his thoughts again.

"When Symphony tried to contact him, his parents told her he was unreachable." Alex sighed,

"He's on some kind of photography mission in some remote place. His parents have been trying without success to reach him since they found out about Symphony and the baby."

"She couldn't contact him…wait…were they not together?" Hope flared in Terry's belly. Maybe, just maybe, he had a chance to get back into Symphony's life once she got better.

Alex cocked a brow at him. "No." She dragged out the word, and Terry could tell she was wondering what he was thinking. "Not since that day in New Orleans."

Terry had no idea. He remembered that a wife popped up out of nowhere, belonging to Kyle. He figured it was some sort of misunderstanding and the two had already worked through all of that.

"So, Kyle's parents are next of kin for the baby and just came and took her from her mother?"

"They waited a few days, but when Symphony was not improving, they needed to head home," Alex stated. "Inheriting a brand-new baby like that…well it calls for an overhaul of your life. They call every day to check on her."

"So, Symphony has no idea that her baby is halfway across the country?"

"No, she doesn't," she said, then straightened in her chair. "Let me get this straight, Mr. Phoenix."

Terry rolled his eyes. He knew something was coming and he wasn't going to like it. But before he could say anything, she continued.

"You were under the impression that Symphony and Kyle were still together, yet here *you* are?"

"So? What's your point?"

"My point is, Terry Phoenix," she punctuated each syllable in his name. "What exactly is your plan? It's been seven months. Had you planned to find out where Symphony was with the hope of breaking up a relationship nearly a year in the making?"

"Yes." His admission held no remorse.

"And now that they have a child together? What's your plan now?"

"My plan is to have Symphony?"

He watched her eyes narrow. He was sure she was about to open her mouth to say something, but he wasn't in the mood for a lecture. He turned away from her and sat back in his seat. Yes, Symphony and Kyle had a child together, but the fact was, they weren't together.

Terry thought about Symphony's reaction to waking up and not being able to put the baby in her arms. After a moment, he looked up toward the television, still swimming in his own thoughts.

After a while, Alex told him she was leaving and that she'd call him later to check to see how Symphony was progressing. Her disheartened eyes told him that she was beginning to lose hope that Symphony would ever recover.

Terry stood and pulled Alex into his arms, even though he was still annoyed with her. He'd never seen his cousin's wife so out of sorts. She'd always been so put together, confident, and in control. "She's going to be ok, Alex. You don't know her like I do." He pulled her away, so she could see his face. "I know she is fighting like hell to get back to her daughter." Alex gave him a watery smile, nodded, and quickly walked away.

Terry finally pulled his cell phone out to check any messages or emails from work as he settled back into the waiting room chair. He saw what seemed like an urgent email from his office manager. The subject line read, 24 HOURS TO CLOSE THE DEAL. Terry was about to call the office when he noticed that Leslie had also tried to text him several times over the past few hours.

What the hell was going on?

He tapped Leslie's name to call her. She picked up immediately.

"Mr. Phoenix!"

"Mr. Phoenix?"

Terry looked up at the nurse hovering over him, trying to get his attention, just as he heard Leslie's relief that he'd finally called.

He stood quickly, holding up a finger for the nurse to give him a nanosecond and spoke to Leslie. "Sorry Leslie, I'll have to call you back."

"But, Mr. Phoenix there's an emer—"

He disconnected the call to focus on the nurse.

"Yes, I'm Terry Phoenix. Is Symphony ok?"

He asked, hoping for good news but bracing himself for the worst.

The nurse beckoned him forward, urgently, but the smile on her face gave him a modicum of relief. "The doctor is in with her now and wishes to speak to you. He wants to talk to her next of kin."

Terry paused briefly.

"Next of kin?"

"Yes, as her fiancé, he will be able to speak to you in more detail about her condition."

Terry had forgotten the lie the previous nurse prompted him to tell in order to visit Symphony in the ICU.

"You are her fiancé, aren't you? There was a sticky note left on the desk next to her chart, listing you as family."

"Yes, I'm sorry. I've just been so worried."

Terry walked toward the room where Symphony was hooked up to the machines, hoping she was finally awake. There was a short, very dark man in scrubs and a white coat. He assumed it was the doctor. He stood just outside of Symphony's door. He walked toward Terry with an expression Terry couldn't place. Terry wasn't sure if he was about to get good or bad news.

"Mr. Phoenix?" The doctor had a very thick accent and stood about five inches shorter than Terry. He thought maybe the accent was Nigerian. The man sounded like a golf buddy of his who was from that country.

"Yes, I'm Terry Phoenix. How is she?"

"I'm Doctor Eze." The man stuck his hand out. Terry gave him a hurried handshake.

"How is she?" Terry asked again, irritated with the pleasantries.

"Well, Mr. Phoenix…" Dr. Eze looked up at Terry with kind dark eyes.

"What is it?"

"She's awake." Terry noted the uneasy tone in which he said this.

"Symphony's high blood pressure caused her to have a stroke."

The pain of hearing those words pushed Terry's eyes closed. He could feel his heart racing. He was certain Symphony had lasting effects from the stroke. "We are not quite sure why the coma lasted so long. Her brain function is—"

Terry's eyes went round, magnifying the terror-stricken look on his face.

"Just be straight with me, Doctor. Is she going to be ok?"

Dr. Eze was not going to let Terry rush him. "As I was saying, her brain function is still normal in all the tests we've performed. Her reflexes, speech, and facial movements are all quite normal as well."

Hope blazed in Terry.

"But—" Dr. Eze continued.

"But what?" It was all Terry could do to keep from shaking the man.

"But she doesn't seem to remember how she got here. She wants to see you though."

Terry was stunned.

"She wants to see *me*?"

"Yes, when I told her that Terry Phoenix, her fiancé, was here, she asked for you."

Terry looked toward the room, and the doctor patted him on the arm. "Go on. But give her time. Don't ask her a lot of questions or force her to remember anything just yet."

Terry took a few steps and stopped. "The baby?"

Dr. Eze shook his head. "I'm sure it will come back to her. I understand the baby is with your parents?"

Terry didn't have time to correct him. He just nodded and steeled himself for his first encounter with Symphony.

He stood in the doorway, just watching her for a moment. How could her condition have improved so drastically in only a few hours? The machine that was helping her breathe was gone. All that remained was the IV tube. Her eyes were closed, but she looked like she was sleeping peacefully.

"Welcome back, sweetheart."

Her lids fluttered open, and the recognition in her watery smiling eyes nearly took his breath away. He wanted to drown in the brown depths of them. He'd not seen such a welcoming look from them in what seemed like a lifetime. She lifted her arms to him, and he didn't hesitate in walking over to her and pulling her into the best embrace he could muster with the hospital bed and railing in his way.

"How're you feeling, Symphony?"

"I'm tired and a little confused. The doctor told me I had a slight stroke. My body hurts everywhere."

"I'm sure you'll be feeling better soon."

"Yes, I hope so. Everything is a little fuzzy."

"Do you know who this man is?" Dr. Eze finally asked as he stepped into the room.

"Of course, I do," Symphony replied, not taking her eyes off Terry.

"Who is he?

"Terry Phoenix."

"How do you know him?"

She smiled up at Terry again. "We fell in love sitting in my aunt's bakery and have been inseparable ever since."

Chapter Four

"But I don't understand how she can't remember being pregnant." Terry paced the corridor between the ICU and the waiting room, his hands locked, resting on his head. The nurses were preparing to move Symphony to a regular room. The medical staff felt she no longer needed intensive care. Terry was baffled. "How could she not remember a life growing inside of her?"

Dr. Eze glanced casually through Symphony's chart. "Mr. Phoenix, I won't tell you that this type of amnesia is common—"

"Amnesia?" Terry cut him off. *Amnesia*. He hadn't really thought about it like that. He stopped and faced the doctor, whose calm demeanor was irritating. "Will she ever remember? Don't you think we should tell her?"

"These things have to be dealt with very carefully, or it could cause other psychological episodes. Amnesia is very tricky and a bit fragile."

"Psychological episodes?"

"Well…Mr. Phoenix, finding out that you can't remember your own baby can be rather traumatic. I would hate for her mind to block out other events in her life as well."

"Won't she wonder about the scar on her belly and why her breasts and belly aren't the way she remembers them?" Terry was really concerned, because all Symphony knew was that she'd been in a coma from a stroke. She only knew that, because the doctor told her.

"Of course, she will have to be told. I'm just saying we must tread carefully at this stage. We will talk to her when she gets settled in the new room."

Terry called Alex and Joshua to tell them that Symphony was awake and was being moved to a regular room. He didn't dare tell them anything other than it appeared she would have a full recovery. He told them that it was best to give her a day or so before they visited. After the call, he headed to the gift shop.

He loaded the counter with small and large plush items, flowers, and whatever else he thought she would like. It felt good to be buying things for Symphony again, and it made him feel almost normal.

"Is there anything else, sir?"

"No thanks," He answered the bubbly cashier. He frowned. She looked too young to be working. "Shouldn't you be in school?"

She giggled and rattled off while she rang up the merchandise, "I'm in the work program at my school. I get to leave the last two periods of the day and come to work. I'm sixteen. Normally there is someone in here with me, but she got sick and had to leave. She said that I've been doing a good enough job, so she felt comfortable leaving me here by myself for a little while. The manager will be here in a little while to be with me, because it gets busy in the evenings when people start getting off work and coming to visit people. Is your wife in the hospital?"

It took Terry a second or two to realize she'd asked him a question. He'd zoned out on her halfway through her spiel. She looked at him with wide expectant eyes.

"Uh…what?" he asked.

"Is your wife in the hospital?"

She held up two of the stuffed animals he'd purchased. They were both holding hearts.

"No, my fiancé."

Terry readily claimed the title and did not think of it as a lie. Symphony would be his whether she knew it or not.

Terry walked down the corridor carrying his gifts for Symphony and turned the corner to see Alex and Joshua enter Symphony's hospital room.

"Oh shit!" he said aloud. How the hell did they get here so quickly? The two nurses at the nurse's station looked up at him. Terry didn't notice. He was worried what the couple may say to Symphony. He hadn't had a chance to talk to them about her memory loss. He wondered again how they'd gotten to the hospital so quickly.

In a few quick strides, Terry entered Symphony's hospital room. She was propped up in bed. No longer was she wearing the faded light blue hospital gown, instead, she wore a soft cotton pink pajama top along with a look of alarm projecting from her eyes.

Symphony's wide eyes and scrunched brows were answered by the confusion hovering between Alex and Joshua. Terry quickly took in all their faces, dumped the items he'd bought on a chair by the window, and went to Symphony's side. She reached for his hand, and Terry saw Alex and Joshua exchange a look before he spoke.

Symphony stared up at him, her eyes waiting, expectantly.

"Symphony, this is my cousin Joshua and his wife Alexandra." She looked toward the couple and gave them a tentative smile.

Reaching up to hold on to Joshua's upper arm, Alexandra's smile faded as she looked from Symphony to Terry, and then up at Joshua. His frown matched hers. Alex looked back at Symphony.

"Symphony?" Alex questioned with a hesitant chuckle.

"Uh, Alex, Joshua…" Terry interrupted "May I speak to you in the hallway a moment?" His eyes fell to Symphony. "There's an urgent business matter I need to discuss with them."

Symphony looked toward the pair. "Do the two of you work with Terry?"

Before they could answer, he ushered them to the door. Terry turned to Symphony held up a finger and mouthed, "One minute." He turned to Alex and Joshua. "Will you two step out into the hallway with me for a moment? Please."

The instant he eased the hospital door closed, Alex turned to him. "What's going on, Terry? She's acting like she doesn't even know us."

Weariness pushed through his pores and consumed him. The words he wanted to say weighed his tongue down. He just let them rest there. Terry didn't have the strength to speak or make any sense of this senseless situation, and he was pretty sure if he tried, it would open a dam that he was trying like hell to keep from spilling over. The distress he saw in Alex's eyes was just one more thing piling against his own heartache. He just turned and walked away.

Chapter Five

Symphony woke when she heard the door of her hospital room open. She was exhausted and hurting all over, especially her belly. It was Dr. Eze. There'd been a different doctor in earlier checking her abdomen, but she remembered Dr. Eze promised to visit with her once she'd moved to a new room. Here she was, in a new room, and all she knew was that she'd had a stroke.

"Ah, Ms. James, I'm sorry if I woke you." The doctor's accent scratched against the silence of the room. It sounded especially foreign to her ears, not only because he wasn't born in the States, but because it wasn't Terry's.

Where was Terry? He walked his cousin and his wife out of the room and never returned. Why was everything so confusing right now?

"Ms. James?" The doctor interrupted her thoughts of Terry.

Symphony pushed the button to lift the bed a bit more. "It's ok." The words came out around a yawn and a hitch of pain from her middle.

Dr. Eze tapped a pen against Symphony's chart. "Your blood pressure is still a little higher than I'd like to see it, but for a person who was just in a coma, I'm quite impressed with how well you've recovered from it." He checked her eyes with a light and had her do all sorts of other things to check who knows what.

"So, does that mean I can go home?"

"I don't see why not." He smiled at her and tucked the penlight in the pocket of his white coat. She smiled brightly. She wanted her own bed. "We'll keep you maybe another night or two, but as long as you stay in the area for a little while, I don't see why you can't recover in a more comfortable bed, at least. I would like to conduct some more neurological tests in a week to make sure there are no long-term side effects.

Stay in the area? Her smile faded. "You're a neurologist?"

Dr. Eze looked around the room. "Where is your fiancé?" She saw his eyes stop on the things piled in the chair.

"He stepped out for a while." When she saw his forehead crease, she stated, "Urgent business." That's all she could assume.

42

"I would really like to have this conversation with the two of you."

"Doctor, I have the right to know what's going on with me. It's my body, not his. Why do you have to do tests on my brain when it's my insides that seem to be the problem?" His hesitation worried her. She frowned. "Was I in some sort of accident? I feel all banged up. I know from the nurses that I've had some sort of surgery."

The nurses had been pretty tight-lipped when they made her walk the hallways before settling her into the new room, helping her with clothes from a bag that she didn't recognize, though the clothes inside were familiar.

The doctor pulled over the empty chair next to the one filled with gift shop items and sat next to the hospital bed.

Oh, it was bad. It was *really* bad. She could feel it. Symphony braced herself for the doctor's words. Since she'd been conscious, she tried to come up with something so bad that could have her in a coma and cause her to have some kind of emergency surgery. She also was frustrated that she couldn't think of what she was doing before she landed in the hospital. And why hadn't her aunt come to see her yet? Maybe she hadn't been notified.

It had to be cancer.

Cancer.

Could it have been eating her alive without her knowing it?

Symphony focused on Dr. Eze's eyes. They had that look that doctors on TV had when they were about to deliver some bad news—detached and serious.

"It's cancer, isn't it? I have cancer? Is that what's wrong with me? I passed out somewhere, you did a scan and had to try to remove it? Is that why I have the scar? You couldn't get it all, could you? It's gotten into my organs? Am I going to die? Just tell me."

He patted her blanket-covered shin and gave her a sympathetic chuckle. "No, dear. You do not have cancer."

"Then what is it?"

Dr. Eze took a deep breath. "A week ago, you were brought to the ER, unresponsive. You'd had a stroke brought on by gestational hypertension."

The words took a moment to process—a week...gestational hypertension.

"I've been here a week?" Before he could answer, she continued, "Wait...I'm confused." She paused again, frowning. She tried to sit up on her own, but the pain pushed her back. "Gestational?" Maybe her intestines were all jacked up. Was that the reason why the nurse made her walk earlier? She'd heard that people with intestine or colon surgery had to walk and pass gas before being released. She was also bleeding. Had she had a hysterectomy? That must be it. "Do I have uterine cancer? Have I had a hysterectomy?" It would explain the pain she was having.

Symphony focused on the doctor again, who was sitting there patiently waiting while she processed the information. She grabbed the side rail. "Just give it to me straight. I promise that my imagination is far worse than whatever you have to say."

So, he told her.

"You were pregnant when you were brought in. Your pregnancy caused a dangerous spike in your blood pressure, resulting in you having a stroke and leaving you unresponsive. An emergency cesarean was performed. The stroke has also left you with amnesia. That is why you do not remember the pregnancy or where you were before you were brought in. I'm fairly certain that your memory will return fully after your body has gotten over this shocking episode."

She just stared at him.

Time slowed.

The room became so devoid of sound that her pulse echoed in her ears like slow vibrating drumbeats. Her lashes slammed together. They were heavy iron vaults. Steel clashing against steel. Again and again.

She was wrong.

This truth was far worse than anything she could imagine.

She could see Dr. Eze's eyes on her expectantly. Hers felt round and dry—stones set in her head. The head that, at the moment, was broken. It was too much. Too much to know. Too harsh to know and much too unreal to comprehend. Symphony's eyes slid closed, and her head turned away from the man sitting at her side. Her hand fell away from the rail. His hand still rested lightly on her shin.

She felt full and empty all at once. Something was missing. Suddenly the weight of her breasts was startling. She crossed her arms over her chest, trying unsuccessfully to hug herself and noticed the stabbing ache in her breasts for the first time.

Pregnancy?

Amnesia?

How could she not remember being pregnant? However, it explained why her body felt so foreign to her and why her breasts and stomach hurt so much.

Cesarean? She'd had a baby. The doctor just told her she'd had a baby.

A baby.

A baby.

She'd had a *baby.*

Symphony's eyes flew open. She looked around the room. Pretty pastels colored the walls. A rocking chair sat not far from the bed. This was a maternity room. A maternity room. A room for women who'd just had a baby.

A baby.

She played the doctors words again. *High blood pressure from pregnancy.* Symphony could feel the storm forming at the depths of her soul into something she couldn't fathom—a truth that she knew would break her in two.

Slowly she turned to the doctor, both of his hands now resting on the chart in his lap.

Her next words fought to get around the shards of glass growing in her throat. "The baby?"

"She—"

"She? A girl?" Hot tears scalded her cheeks.

"Yes."

Her eyes closed as she tried to continue to breathe and gather courage for the next question. There was no way she could make herself form the words. *Is she dead or alive?* So, instead, she asked, "Is she here?"

"No, Symphony, I'm sorry. The stroke and coma—"

Dr. Eze's words were halted by what sounded like two gunshots from the other side of the door.

Bang!

Bang!

Then screams and chaos moved the doctor from her side. He shouted back at Symphony for her to get up and lock herself in the bathroom.

She heard nothing past the word, "No."

Chapter Six

London, England

Unfortunately, war zones were not foreign to Kyle Dean. He'd experienced things that he prayed most people would never have to. Once a person had smelled burning flesh, Kyle was certain it could never be forgotten. The acrid stink of burned hair was the only comparison he could make with the smell, yet it was so much worse—gut churning and forbidding.

The eerie silence right before hell unleashed on unsuspecting towns constantly echoed at the core of him, and Kyle sure as hell would never rid himself of the sour taste of fear. At times, it coated him so completely he was left immobile, or sometimes blindly reckless. However, those things were all miniscule in comparison to seeing the lack of hope in a child's eyes.

A child who owned only the dust of debris he carried in his pores. A child whose hands ached to hold the hand of a parent, a sister, a brother, or even a friend that he would never see again. He'd witnessed hundreds, maybe even thousands of children with slim chances of hope to grow up to be healthy, happy, and free from torment, oppression, fear, and poverty. Kyle could lock his heart away from lots of things, but a suffering child, damaged in every way imaginable, was what nightmares were made of.

He tossed his gear on the bed. For the past two months, he'd carried a backpack with the barest essentials to survive the dangerous elements he faced, in addition to a bag that carried his photography equipment. With the mission completed, Kyle was armed with a plane ticket home and an ample bank account that reflected the danger he endured as well as the great shots he'd captured.

Kyle was not sorry he'd gone. What was happening in the Middle East was something the world needed to know in more intimate details than the media provided. Kyle was only sorry that for the past two months he'd had no contact with anyone in the States. Even if it worked, the cell phone he'd brought with him had long since been traded for clean water and food. Now, his mission was getting Symphony back, and just like his latest one, it would be successful.

First, he needed a shower.

Just a turn of a knob and the steaming water flowed freely. He stood there a moment just letting the stream flow through his fingers, thinking of the many nights he wished he could wash away the grit of the day and the stench of huddling with so many unwashed bodies hovering beneath the stones of a fallen bridge or some other makeshift shelter, while armed murderers looked to massacre the few who'd gotten away.

Kyle forced those thoughts away and focused his thoughts on Symphony. He wondered what she was doing. It was three months shy of a year since he'd seen her, and it felt like an eternity. He'd been away from her longer than he'd actually known her, but it felt as though Symphony had been a part of his life forever.

He stepped out of the shower, dried, and put on the robe provided by the hotel. There was a knock at his door, and he hoped it was someone bringing the items he'd requested from the shop. He didn't have the strength to shop on his own, so he gave the concierge the details of what he needed, including a piece of luggage to carry it in.

The bellman stood on the other side of the door wearing a crisp smile and suit, towing a suitcase and carrying three shopping bags and a garment bag draped over his arm.

"I've gotten everything you requested, sir." He stated with a lisp in a British accent. Which was odd. Kyle had never heard an accented lisp before and thought about it a moment as he helped the man place the items in the room.

"Thanks." He handed the young bellman a grossly large tip. He figured he deserved it for having to pick out underwear for him.

"Thank you, sir." The man was about to walk back out when Kyle thought of something.

"Hey, can you do me a favor…uh…" Kyle looked at the tag on his coat. "Augustine."

"Anything, sir! And everyone just calls me Gus."

Gus looked to be about twenty-three, and with the way his hair kept flopping in his face, Kyle could tell the stuffy suit was not his first choice of attire. Nevertheless, he still appeared quite professional in his demeanor.

"Do you have a cell phone on you?"

Gus's brows bunched. "We aren't allowed to have our cell phones on duty, sir."

Kyle tilted his head, and his own blond hair would have flopped in his eye if it hadn't been wet from the shower. "That's not what I asked, now, is it?"

The bellman looked a little uncomfortable for a moment before reaching into his pocket and producing a cell phone.

"I'm traveling with limited gear, as you can see, and I don't have my phone. Of course, I know only my parents' number by heart and my girlfriend's, of course, but I need to call my lawyer, and don't have his card. Will you look up a number for Attorney Jackson Jeffries, in Jacksonville, Florida?"

"Why, yes, sir." He punched in the information and was soon giving Kyle the numbers he needed to reach Jackson.

Kyle pulled out more bills for Gus, but he waved them away. Kyle made him take them anyway. "Thanks for all your help, Gus."

"My pleasure, Mr. Dean. I'm here all night if you need anything else."

Kyle didn't plan on needing anything except sleep, but he assured Gus that he would call and ask for him personally if he needed anything.

Kyle looked at the hotel phone and read the instructions to make an international call. He hadn't used a phone in a hotel in years, if ever. He was surprised hotels still provided them, since everyone had cell phones, but he was glad they did.

It was about four p.m. in Florida. Jackson's cell number wasn't listed on his website, but he hoped he forwarded calls there if he was out of the office. Kyle was in luck. Jackson was in. After telling his secretary who he was, he was quickly connected to Jackson.

"Damn it, Kyle, I've been trying to reach you for a couple weeks! Where are you?"

"I've just traveled through hell to get to London. I'm heading home tomorrow. I told you it might be impossible to reach me." Kyle had left numbers to several rendezvous points for emergencies.

"I know…I know."

"Is Shelia still causing trouble? For the life of me, man, I don't know what happened to her. This isn't the Shelia I grew up with. Is there another issue with the divorce?"

"There is no need for a divorce now."

Kyle frowned. "Why not?"

"She's dead."

"What?" His heart pumped faster in his chest. What was Jackson talking about? Who was dead? Had something happened to Symphony?

And before his mind and heart tipped over the cliff, Jackson said, "Shelia. Shelia's dead, Kyle."

Even though she'd been a pain in his ass and caused a serious misunderstanding between Symphony and him, the news of Shelia's death struck him hard.

"Shelia's dead? What happened to her?"

"Overdose. Some cleaning lady found her in one of those fancy hotels in the Quarter."

Kyle leaned back against the headboard. "What?"

"The news article indicated she was a prostitute. The man who signed for the room was questioned, booked for soliciting a prostitute, and as far as I know, was released. The man claimed they had sex, he paid her, and he left. He told her she could stay in the room until morning. Didn't seem to be any foul play."

Shelia was dead. The girl from next door who kept their secrets when her brother and he snuck out at night. The girl who told his parents that he'd gotten in trouble at school, because she knew he would get grounded and not be able to go with her brother and some other boys to break into Jilly's Convenience Store. That lie saved his life. Her brother and one of the other boys were shot and killed. Shelia was now dead too. The girl who he'd married because she needed medical treatments to save her life.

"Kyle? You all right, man?"

"No." Both men were silent. "What happened to her?" he whispered. "To her body?"

"The police found my card in her purse and called me. Asked if I knew any of her family. From what you'd told me, I knew her parents were dead, so technically, you were her only relative. On your behalf, I provided the money needed to cremate her. There was no service."

"Thanks for doing that."

"I knew you would have done it yourself."

Jackson was right. He would have done the same. He hated that Shelia went down the path that she did. He could have helped her more. He *would* have helped her. Why hadn't he done more to find out about her? Several years ago, she'd gotten in touch with him and told him that she was better and thanked him for what he'd done. After that, he'd stopped putting her on his paperwork, and no one ever questioned his new status or asked to see any documents stating he was divorced.

"So…what's next for you?"

"I'll be in Florida to see my parents for a few days, and then I'm going to find my girl. I know Symphony. She can't stay away from her business too long."

"Good luck, Dean. Let me know if I can help in any way."

"Don't worry, I will. And thanks for your help with Shelia."

Kyle disconnected the phone. He thought about calling his parents, but he wasn't in the mood to talk to anyone. He'd see them tomorrow when he got back to Daytona. His flight left first thing in the morning, and he couldn't wait.

Chapter Seven

The house sat there, paint faded and chipped, grass overgrown—unkempt and empty. Like Shelia was before she died. The house was so unlike he remembered it as a kid. The neighborhood, just blocks from the ocean, was once vibrant and lively with kids playing in the street—kids with two-parent families. Now, all the kids were grown and most gone from the neighborhood. Only a few of the original homeowners were left. His parents were now surrounded by retirees and what they called "yuppies with no ambition except to surf and work just enough to be able to pay rent."

For some reason, Shelia's home had been empty for quite some time. Kyle's dad told him that an older married couple bought it years ago after Shelia's family moved away. Their long-time neighbors had moved not long after Nick, Shelia's brother and his best friend, died. The new family never did anything with the house nor wanted to sell it. His dad figured it was someone who had a plan to move out to the beach one day, but for some reason, never had.

"Sir?" The cab driver captured his attention and pointed to the meter.

"Oh, sorry." Kyle reached in his pocket, handed the man money, grabbed his bags, and got out of the cab. He saw his SUV in the driveway in front of the garage. He knew his mom was probably using it as he'd suggested before he left so it wouldn't just sit idle.

He peeked inside. What was a car seat doing in there? He looked at the backseat and saw a few toys laying there. Kyle was still puzzled when he knocked on the front door before using his key to open it. He dropped his bags near the entrance and went in pursuit of his parents.

"Mom! Why is there a car seat in the back of my car?" There was no one in the family room. "Mom! Dad! Where are you?" It was ten a.m. They were usually up long ago, so he was sure they weren't asleep. He headed for the stairs. "Mom!" he yelled again. His mom came running toward the stairs, finger pressed against her lips, dressed in sweatpants and a Mickey Mouse T-shirt. Her hair was not perfectly in place like it usually was. She was in her late fifties and still looked great, and so did his dad, but he'd only seen her dressed like this when she wasn't feeling well.

"Shhhh!"

"Mom, are you sick?" he whispered.

"Kyle?" Her hands covered her mouth as she ran down the stairs to meet him. "Kyle! You're home. You're finally home."

Her embrace was fierce. He held her and felt her tremble.

"Mom, I'm ok. Are you crying?" His mom was not a crier. "Mom." He pushed away from her to look at her face. His voice was softer with concern. "Mom? What's wrong? You never acted like this when I returned home from my tours in the Army."

She grabbed him again and sobbed. "Oh Kyle, we're so glad you're home…Warren!" she called out without yelling. She pulled Kyle away from the stairs. "Let's go in here. The baby is sleeping."

"Baby? What Baby? I saw the car seat in my SUV. Whose baby do you have, and why?"

She ignored his questions.

"Warren!" she called out again.

His dad must have been in the laundry room, because he stepped into the family room from the kitchen holding a small laundry basket of clothes.

Kyle saw the baby clothes. "What's going on, guys. You two have another baby and didn't tell me?"

His dad put the basket on the floor and grabbed his son. "Oh, it's good to see you, son. Didn't you get any of the messages we left for you?"

His dad's eyes were glassy. "Dad?" Warren pulled him back into an embrace. "Dad, I'm here. I'm fine." His mom joined in the hug. Kyle's throat was tightening. He'd never seen his parents like this. They'd always been a loving family, but he hadn't seen this type of emotion out of them in a very long time, if ever.

"I didn't get your messages. All of our rendezvous spots were raided and destroyed. They were trying to knock out all unauthorized communications in the area." He didn't try to explain who the "they" were. In the long run, it didn't really matter. "Why were you trying to reach me?"

"Come, let's sit," his mom said.

Kyle saw his dad look toward the stairs.

"She's asleep," his mom told him.

Warren nodded and sat on the sofa next to his wife. Kyle sat next to them and waited.

"Were you trying to reach me to tell me about Shelia?"

"Shelia? Shelia Duncan, from next door?" his mom asked.

"This isn't about Shelia?" Kyle asked, confused.

Warren looked at his wife and back at Kyle. "We haven't seen or heard from Shelia since they moved away. Have you?"

"Yes." Kyle stated, still wondering what this was all about, but he told them about his marriage to Shelia, and why, and about her subsequent death.

"My God," his mom exclaimed with her hand on her chest. "Why didn't you tell us any of this before?"

"Honestly Mom, I hadn't thought about it in a while, and at the time I married her, I didn't think it was a big deal because it wasn't a 'real' marriage. Shelia just happened to show up when Symphony and I arrived in New Orleans. It's also the reason Symphony left, and why I haven't heard from her since."

His parents looked at each other again. Their eyes were speaking more words than what they were saying, which was nothing.

"That was the last time you talked to her? So, you didn't know she was—"

"Wait...*you've* talked to her?" Kyle stood. "You've talked to Symphony?"

"Not exactly, son." It was his father who spoke then.

"Do you know where she is?"

His parents looked at each other again and uneasiness squeezed Kyle's insides. "Do you know where she is?"

His mom nodded.

Hope ignited in his chest. "Where is she?"

"She's in Baton Rouge. Her friend, the lawyer, lives there."

"Alexandra?"

"Yes, that's her name."

"Symphony is in Baton Rouge with Alex?" He stood again and paced back and forth.

"Sit down, Kyle," his dad quietly commanded.

Kyle sat, rubbing his hands down his face. He knew where she was. Now all he had to do was go there and talk some sense into her.

Wait…

"How do the two of you know where she is? Did she contact you while I was gone? Was she trying to reach me?"

His mom reached for his dad's hand. "Tell him, Warren."

Kyle looked slowly from his mom to his dad. "Tell me what?"

At that moment, he heard a baby's cry through a monitor on the end table that he'd not noticed before.

"Why do you have a baby in the house? Whose baby is it?"

"Yours," they said in unison.

Chapter Eight

He couldn't have heard them correctly. "What?" He was about to laugh, but they both looked so serious.

"Pixie, you may as well get her since she seems to be up." His mom's name was Margret, but everyone called her Pixie.

Kyle watched his mom hurry toward the stairs. He turned back to his dad. "Dad, what's this all about?" The baby's cry softened to a whimper.

"Come on, sweetie. Your daddy is finally home," he heard his mom say through the monitor.

"Dad, what's going on?" He stressed each word.

"Symphony's friend, Alex, contacted us."

"Why?"

"Apparently, Symphony left documents for you in case something went wrong."

"What do you mean, 'in case something went wrong'?"

"With the pregnancy."

"Symphony's pregnant?"

"You didn't know?"

"No. I told you I hadn't seen her since that day in New Orleans." Kyle ran his hands through his hair. He looked at the ceiling as if he could see through it. "Dad?"

"Let me finish, so you can understand."

Kyle's mind was whirling. Why hadn't she told him? Was the baby from someone else...Terry? Then everything from seeing the car seat to hearing what his mom said through the monitor hit him with the force of a tsunami.

He stared at his dad, his heart racing.

His dad continued, "Let me first say that Alex called yesterday and said Symphony seems to be recovering."

"What happened to her, Dad?"

"The pregnancy caused her blood pressure to spike, and she slipped into a coma."

"A coma." The words were barely audible.

"When they couldn't get you, they contacted your mom and me. After she'd been in the coma nearly a week, we were left with no choice but to bring Cadence home. We've only been back a couple of days"

"Cadence?"

"That's her name. Cadence Alexandra Dean. She's your daughter, Kyle."

66

Just then, his mom walked in with a baby in her arms. She was clad in a pink onesie and was a miniature version of Symphony. She was beautiful. Her hair, more like his than her mom's, was so blonde that it was a soft glowing halo of curls on her sweet little perfect head. Kyle was instantly in love with her.

He couldn't move.

His mom sat on the edge of the coffee table, so he could see her more clearly. He automatically reached for her, and her blue eyes looked at him like she knew that from now on, he would be her protector, savior, and hero.

This was *his* daughter. He and Symphony created this beautiful tiny human. She was a tiny little person that was a part of him—belonged to him.

Symphony.

It suddenly hit him that the only reason a new baby wouldn't be with its mom is because there was something seriously wrong. His dad's words came back to him. *High blood pressure. A coma—for a week.*

Kyle looked down at his daughter, quietly staring up at him. He touched her hands and each foot—ten perfect fingers and ten perfect little toes. He knew he was stalling, but he wasn't quite ready for the reason why Cadence was here with his parents and not her mother.

Cadence. And just like that, she had her own identity and was no longer, *the baby.*

"She's such a sweetheart…hardly ever cries."

"Thanks, Mom." She gave him a watery smile. "Dad…" Kyle looked at his father, "thank you guys for taking care of her."

"Your mom had the time of her life shopping."

Kyle looked around and noticed baby stuff everywhere. Did babies really need all this stuff?

"The doctors say she's going to be all right, son." Kyle's gaze wouldn't move from the colorful baby seat across from him. "Symphony is out of danger."

His dad's words were the balm he needed. Kyle's shoulders shook, and the tears fell, unchecked. His mom reached to take Cadence, but he couldn't let her go. He had to hold on to her—hold on to the hope she represented, that he could make Symphony love him again.

Chapter Nine

Why had he left her? He didn't know what the hell was going on. It had been four hours. Part of the hospital was on lockdown, and other parts had been evacuated. Alex, Joshua, and Terry were on the outskirts of the parking lot where visitors were instructed to wait. He knew something was very wrong by all the activity that was going on outside. News crews from the area, and even as far as New Orleans, had arrived and were covering the story. Nothing had been confirmed, but people from inside the hospital were contacting others through texts and Facebook about shots being fired in the hospital. The reporters were gathering information any way they could get it and speculating on what may have happened.

"Did the doctor say how long the amnesia would last? Is there anything that can be done to help her get her memory back?" Alex still couldn't believe Symphony didn't know who she was. "Should we call to tell the Deans what's going on?"

"*We* don't even know what's going on," Terry snapped.

"We know you're upset, Cuz, but there's no need to take it out on my wife."

"No, it's ok, Joshua. I know he's upset. We all are."

Terry wasn't in the mood for questions or apologies. He'd stopped a police officer a few minutes before, telling him that his fiancé was in the hospital, but that he needed information. Terry looked around and made his way near one of the reporters. She was on live.

"This just in from one of our viewers who knows someone who works in the hospital. Apparently, the shooting stemmed from a domestic situation. A spouse walked in a room on the maternity ward floor and shot his wife and at least one other person. There may have been others shot, but we can't confirm the number or their conditions as of yet."

This was a nightmare. All of this. He just wanted to wake up and find himself still in college with the girl of his dreams.

After another hour, all visitors were told that nonessential personnel were not allowed to reenter the hospital. They would have to come back tomorrow. The only information they were given was that the family of the injured were notified, and everyone else on the maternity floor was moved to another part of the hospital. The trio took some relief in the news. They could only assume Symphony was safe.

***

Symphony vaguely remembered Dr. Eze helping her to the bathroom. It was the only door in the room that locked. He wouldn't leave the door until he'd heard it lock. She didn't know how long she'd been in there. Her thoughts were on the baby that was lost to her.

She'd sat mostly on the bath seat in the shower until Dr. Eze told her to come out. An officer had already told her it was safe to come out, but she didn't trust a voice she didn't know. She hadn't really known if she'd really been in danger. It didn't matter. Nothing mattered.

"Ms. James, we're moving you to another floor."

"Why?"

The nurses looked at each other. "Because of the shooting, ma'am."

"Ok." She didn't care. "Where is the doctor? He's ok, right?" She hadn't thought to ask when she came out of hiding.

"Yes, ma'am. I believe he's either still speaking to the police or has gone home," one of them replied. She didn't know which because she'd closed her eyes.

Once she was settled in the new room, she wondered again where Terry was. Symphony pushed the button to call the nurse.

"Yes, ma'am?" the crackled voice asked.

"Will my fiancé know where I am?"

"Yes, ma'am." Symphony heard her mumble something that sounded like, "Oh here it is…Baby Dean."

"When visitors are allowed to return tomorrow, Mr. Dean will be informed of your new room number."

"Mr. Dean?" She didn't get a reply. She didn't have the energy to question or challenge the mistake; Symphony simply leaned back in the bed and cried.

Sometime during the night Symphony fell asleep. Her dreams were filled with flashes of her in a bakery that she'd never seen before but felt oddly familiar. She felt happy in her dreams. Flashes of a blond man plagued her all night. She dreamed of crying in his arms and feeding him pastries. *Kyle Dean is that you?* She heard the woman say, and she awoke with a start.

"I'm sorry, Ms. James. I need to take your blood pressure."

"I don't know if it's a good time. My heart is racing."

The nurse felt her pulse and asked if she was ok. She told her that she'd just had a weird dream and was startled awake.

"I'll let you settle down for about twenty minutes and come back," the nurse said sweetly before leaving the room.

Symphony was grateful. She wanted to get out of there and knew the doctor wouldn't let her go if her blood pressure didn't settle down. She took some deep breaths and tried not to think of the dream she'd had. After a while, the nurse came back and was satisfied with Symphony's blood pressure and other vitals. She checked her abdomen and asked Symphony about the pain. The pain in her abdomen was nothing compared to the ache in her heart.

Is that why Terry was having a difficult time facing her? Was he upset with her for losing the baby? And why couldn't she remember anything? She didn't even know what hospital she was in. She was pretty sure since she'd been in a coma, they'd probably brought her to Jacksonville. St. Augustine's hospital wasn't small, but it wasn't very large either.

Why hadn't her aunt been here? The flash of her crying in the man's arms came back to her, and she felt the grief of a great loss. Symphony eased out of bed. She found her bag in the closet and carefully placed it on one of the chairs. She'd still not looked at all the stuff Terry had brought in; he hadn't been back. She opened the bag and dug through it until she found her phone. It wasn't familiar, but somehow, she knew it was hers. She felt like if she could find something familiar, everything else would settle into place.

She also knew the blond man was important. Why did she know Terry but couldn't remember anything else? She was certain the couple that came in with him knew her. She knew she was supposed to know them as well. Why couldn't she remember?

She settled back in the bed, having found that moving around was getting easier, if still a little painful. When she touched the circle on the phone, it came to life, but the battery was very low. She went to the address book and found several contacts with the last name Phoenix—but not Terry's contact information. She was surprised to see Joshua Phoenix and Alexandra Phoenix's phone number, email, and an address in Boston. She scrolled to the D's, and there it was, the name "Kyle Dean."

Who was he?

She clicked on the pictures. There were several pictures of her pregnant. She couldn't stop the tears that fell.

There were no pictures of Terry. She saw pictures of the lady—Alex.

From the looks of the pictures, they were friends.

Friends.

Why couldn't she remember her? It was so frustrating. Symphony clicked on an album titled "Kyle." There were picture after picture of the man in her dream. The two of them in places she recognized. "That's at the top of the lighthouse!" she said aloud. There was a picture of the two of them sitting in a bakery.

"That's my shop! I own that bakery!"

The phone went black. "Damn it!" She didn't remember seeing a charger. Symphony eased her legs out of the bed again. It was still early; the sun hadn't made an appearance yet. She went to the bathroom to take care of her needs, hating the thick pads she had to wear. When everything was in place, she found her slippers in the bag and walked out of the room.

"Ms. James," one of the nurses called out, "are you ok?"

"Is there a place I can use a computer?"

"No ma'am, patients aren't authorized to come back here."

Symphony leaned on the counter. "Please, it's important."

The nurse looked around. She was the only one at the station. "I have my personal laptop." Symphony brightened for the first time since the talk with Dr. Eze. "I was using it to finish up one of my college assignments. I'm getting my masters. Come on, honey, let's get you back in bed. You can use it in there."

"Thank you. Thank you so much." Symphony noticed the woman's dialect. "Are you from Louisiana?"

"Yes, ma'am. Born and raised here." She placed her hand on Symphony's arm to steady her.

Symphony stared at the woman, "Here?"

"Yeah, m'baby, I grew up not too far from here."

"Are you telling me I'm in Louisiana?"

The nurse looked at Symphony a long time. Her eyes widened. "You're the patient with amnesia."

"That's what they keep telling me."

The nurse looked around again as if she was breaking more rules. She helped Symphony in bed. "We were instructed not to ask you any questions, but since you asked me…yes, ma'am, you're in Baton Rouge, Louisiana."

How in the hell did she get here?

She'd get to her current situation later. Right now she wanted to find out more about her bakery.

For the next hour, Symphony was busy on the computer gathering information about her bakery. Her reviews were great. There were several comments from tourists who wished there was a Symphony's in their town. From what she'd found out, she was pretty sure she still lived in Florida.

The nurse soon finished up her night shift and needed her computer, but Symphony had a better idea of where she was, who she was, and where she lived. Now, her objective was to find out why she was halfway across the country.

Chapter Ten

The moment they were accepting visitors, he was there. Terry couldn't wait to see her. He didn't know if she was worried something happened to him, or if she was scared, or if she had somehow suffered a setback from all of this.

She was crying when he walked in. "Symphony, what's wrong?"

"The doctor told me what happened. I can't stop crying."

What did the doctor tell her that had her crying? Was she just upset that she didn't remember the pregnancy?

"It'll be ok, Symphony. I'm just glad you're safe."

"I don't remember any of it, Terry. How can I not remember being pregnant?"

"I'm sure it'll come back."

"I don't want it to come back. Then I'd just have to relive it all over again."

Terry wondered if the pregnancy had been that awful that she wouldn't want to remember her daughter growing inside of her.

"Where were you?" she asked. "I was worried."

Terry wondered how much the doctor told her about her condition. He assumed he'd mentioned it since she commented on not remembering. "I'm sorry I wasn't here with you during all of that yesterday." He pulled up a chair and took her hand in his. "I needed to talk to Alex and Joshua. They weren't aware of the amnesia."

"I know them, don't I?"

"Yes."

"I knew it." She sounded relieved.

"You've been staying at Alex's home, here in Baton Rouge."

"Why?"

What was he supposed to tell her? That she was hiding from him and Dean?

"Why was I staying with her, Terry? I found out last night that I own a bakery in St. Augustine. Why would I leave it to stay in Louisiana? Where were you during all of that time?"

She had a right to know. The one thing he had going for him was that she remembered him and no one else.

"Excuse me, Ms. James?" The man walking in held up a badge. "We have a few questions for you."

Terry turned and stood when he saw the man walk in. "What's this all about?" he asked the man.

"We have a few questions for Ms. James. Who are you?"

"I'm Terry Phoenix."

"What is your relationship to Ms. James?"

The officer and Symphony looked at Terry, waiting for an answer. "I'm her fiancé."

Terry glanced at Symphony and saw something flash in her eyes, but it was so brief he could have imagined it.

The officer turned to Symphony. "Ms. James, we have a few questions for you about the shooting yesterday."

"I don't know what help I can be. I never left my room." Both men were staring at her. It was Terry's first time hearing an account of what happened.

"I was in here talking to Dr. Eze. He'd just given me some terrible news, so I'm really not sure what happened after that. She paused, her forehead creasing. "I think there were two gunshots. He helped me get into the bathroom and wouldn't leave until he heard the door lock. The next thing I knew, a man was telling me it was safe to come out. I didn't come out until I heard Dr. Eze's voice. I didn't know the man

80

was a cop." She looked apologetic before continuing. "They moved me to another room. I don't even know what happened. I haven't looked at the news."

The officer looked at Terry and back at Symphony. "Do either of you know why this man," he pulled a mug shot of a man from his pocket, "would have the name and picture of Ms. James?"

Symphony's breath hitched in surprise.

"What!" Terry exclaimed. "Who is that man, and, I'm sorry, but who exactly are *you*?"

The man turned to Terry. "I'm Detective Vic Sanchez." He then faced Symphony. "This man is Nick Thurman."

Terry cut him off. "Is he the shooter?"

"No. He was killed yesterday by the shooter." Terry could see Symphony getting visibly upset. Her eyes were wide and fixed on the detective. She seemed to be paralyzed and in a state of shock. He squeezed her hand. The detective continued. "As far as we know, he was just a visitor to the hospital. Until—"

Symphony began to tremble.

"Look, this isn't a good time. She can't have anything upsetting her right now."

"It's ok, Detective," Symphony said, finally speaking. "He's just concerned because my brain is broken."

Sanchez raised an eyebrow.

"Terry, it's ok. I need to know what's going on…"

"Symphony, you've already had such a shock. Let me speak to the detective and find out what's going on."

"No! I need to know what's going on." She looked toward Sanchez again. "The man in the picture was shot yesterday. Why?"

"We aren't sure why. There doesn't seem to be any connection between Thurman and the shooter. The shooting, as far as we know, was a domestic situation."

"Domestic?" They both asked.

"Yes, that's all I'm at liberty to say at this point. However, Thurman was shot not far from your hospital room door."

Terry's gut twisted in hearing how close Symphony was to such violence. "And you say he had Symphony's photo in his pocket? Did he have a weapon?"

"No. That's why we think the shooting isn't connected to this guy."

"Why are you so certain?" Terry asked.

"Because Thurman was a once-convicted hitman. He was recently released from prison."

"So why don't you think it's connected?" Terry questioned the officer—his irritation was plain from his tone and the scowl on his face.

"It's not Thurman's style to make such a mess." Silence hung heavily over them after the detective's words.

"Do you think he was coming to harm me?"

"We don't know. So, back to my original question, is there a reason someone may be looking for you?"

Symphony's questioning eyes were fixed on him. They were also filled with frustration at having to depend on others for information about herself. Terry knew Dean was probably looking for her but didn't believe he would have any reason to harm her. Plus, he was off God knows where.

The detective looked from Symphony to Terry. "Is there something I should know?"

"Almost a year ago, she was nearly assaulted by a man who tried to blackmail her." He smiled, "But she actually ended up kicking the guy's ass. He didn't know she'd been taking kickboxing for years." Terry glanced at Symphony to gauge her reaction. There was shock on her face, but also thoughtful concentration, like she was trying to remember. He looked at Sanchez. "The man was working for one of those huge

83

frozen food companies and used unscrupulous tactics when she refused to sell her recipes to them."

"Recipes?" Sanchez scribbled on a notepad. He was more interested in the case now.

"I own a bakery." Both Terry and Sanchez looked at Symphony.

"You remember?" Terry asked cupping her face.

"I was looking through my phone…at pictures…I decided to search the internet."

"Am I missing something?" Detective Sanchez asked.

"That's why I was telling you it's not a good time. She's just woke from a coma and is recovering from a stroke. Her memory is not…completely intact."

"I see."

Terry was pretty sure that the detective saw nothing.

"Is there any reason why someone would want to harm you, other than recipes? What's the name of the bakery?"

"Symphony's," she stated. Terry smiled down at her.

The detective asked several more questions about the incident in South Carolina with the assault. She'd been there for her aunt's funeral, but he didn't disclose that bit of information. Terry did the best that he could to not give it away that he only had secondhand knowledge. He really didn't know much about Symphony's current life since he hadn't been in it. This all was beginning to feel like a lie, and he wondered how she would feel when her memory finally returned. He was sure it would return soon. Symphony was a fighter, and she would fight to get her life back.

***

"That idiot! How the hell did he mess up such a simple job? He wasn't supposed to go and get himself killed. It was supposed to be a warning. A simple warning, and he goes and gets himself shot." The man paced in the cramped motel room, ranting in frustration. He'd finally found her at the same time some fucking idiot decided to go and shoot his wife.

At least before the bastard was killed he verified that Symphony was on the maternity floor. He had to get his hands on that baby.

He had to think.

Maybe Thurman getting shot wasn't such a bad thing. He had the information he needed without having anyone know he was on her trail.

One Choice Away

Everything would fall into place.

Chapter Eleven

Through the detective's interview, Symphony found out a lot about her life. The odd thing was, though she still didn't remember the things Terry told the detective, they didn't seem unfamiliar either. It was like the memories were right there, but she couldn't reach far enough to grasp them.

The only thing that didn't seem real was the loss of her daughter. She hadn't talked about it since her conversation with Dr. Eze. There'd been one interruption after another. She needed to find out what happened to her baby. She'd carried her to term. What had happened? She hadn't seen Dr. Eze, nor had she had an opportunity to fully talk to Terry about how she'd ended up in Baton Rouge. The detective wanted him to tell him more about the incident in Charleston. And then a CT tech had come in to get her for a CT scan before she could be considered for release.

She'd been back in the room for more than an hour when there was a soft knock on the door. It was Alexandra Phoenix.

"Hi, Symphony. Is it ok that I come in?" Symphony smiled. She was glad to see her. She seemed familiar too, but at the very least, she was hoping Alex could fill in the big gaps for her. She still didn't really know much.

"Sure."

Alex's apprehension was etched in her movements. Symphony could tell the woman didn't know how to respond. Alex wore the prettiest teal blue fitted sundress on her tiny frame. "I know we're friends."

"You do?"

"Yes. I saw pictures of the two of us on my phone."

Alex reached into her matching blue bag. "Oh. By the way, I have your charger."

"Great, my phone is dead."

Alex looked around and saw it sitting on the bedside table. "I'll plug it in."

"Thanks."

"I brought your favorite," Alex said, holding up a bag Symphony hadn't noticed.

Symphony was suddenly hungry when she smelled the food. "Cane's!"

"Yep."

"With an extra piece of toast?" she blurted out of nowhere.

"Yes…" Alex looked surprised. "You remember?"

"Yeah, I think I do." Symphony knew there wasn't a Cane's in Florida, but she knew without a doubt there would be four chicken strips, fries, sauce, coleslaw, and two pieces of toast in the bag.

"Ms. James, the doctor has signed your release papers. I just need your signature on these documents."

Both ladies looked up at the nurse in purple scrubs who walked in with paperwork.

"I'm being released?"

Symphony was glad, but she had no idea what to do from there.

"Looks like I came right on time," Alex announced with a smile.

Symphony couldn't help but smile back. She liked Alex. She could tell right away that Alex was really her friend. She could feel it. "Where's Terry?"

"Joshua saw him in the waiting room and almost had to drag him out of here. They went to the small satellite office here in town."

"They have an office here?"

"Yes, we're here quite a bit, and the other guys spend time here as well. Candice grew up here, too, so she and Landon both spend a lot of time in Baton Rouge, too. They visit her parents often."

"Candice and Landon?"

Alex looked embarrassed for a moment. "I'm sorry, Symphony...Landon is my husband Joshua's brother, and Candice is his wife and my best friend. Your friend too."

"And I know these people?"

"Yes, you met them at Ethan and Sophia's reception, almost a year ago." Before Symphony could ask, Alex explained. "Ethan is Landon and Joshua's half-brother. They just found out about him...long story...and Sophia is one of Landon's good friends, who Ethan fell in love with." Symphony must have looked lost in the sea of explanations, because Alex gently took one of her hands and said, "It'll come back to you, Symphony. You just need to see Cadence."

Symphony's heart fluttered at the mention of that name. *I thought her name was Candice*, she thought to herself, and was just about to ask when Dr. Eze walked in.

She was glad to confirm the man had not gotten hurt in the madness of yesterday. "Ms. James, I had not planned on releasing you until tomorrow or the next day, but maybe this is not such a relaxing place for you to try to regain your memory?"

"I agree," Alex chimed in.

"Ah, the lovely Mrs. Phoenix. I assume you will take charge of Ms. James?"

"Yes, Doctor. She's in good hands."

The doctor was immediately called away, so Symphony did not get a chance to ask him any more questions. He did leave instructions with the nurse for when he wanted to see her again.

Symphony was grateful that Alex was so willing to take her in, but she was apprehensive. She worried about the conversation she'd had with the detective earlier. Would her presence put Alex and her family at risk?

Alex would not hear of Symphony not coming home with her. She assured her they all would be safe, and she would, in fact, be safer at their home than anywhere else. A hotel was not an option.

Carla Faye, the housekeeper, brought her a tray laden with food she would never be able to finish. She was still full from the food Alex brought to the hospital.

"It's so wonderful to see you, Ms. Symphony. I've been trying out some of the recipes you've shared with me, and Mr. Briggs can't stop eating them, especially those lemon puffs." She sat the tray on the bed. "He's gained about five pounds but swears his pants have always been that tight." There was well over five pounds of food currently on her tray.

Symphony smiled at the woman. She felt recognition in her heart, but her mind would not let her remember her kind brown face or sharing recipes with her. Clearly, she must have been someone she liked a lot—and trusted—to have given her recipes to her.

"I'll be back soon to get the tray."

Symphony's eyes widened, and her forehead creased.

"You need to eat something, to get your strength back up." Carla Faye chuckled softly, patted Symphony on the shoulder, and walked out the room.

Symphony looked at the tray piled with food and then toward Alex. Both ladies stared at the tray that a room full of grown men couldn't possibly finish and burst into laughter.

After Symphony picked at a few of the dishes on the tray, she settled in the room that she'd obviously used before. Now, she hoped she could finally indulge her curiosity. They made small talk for a while.

"Alex, I get that we're friends, but can you explain to me why I'm in Baton Rouge and not at my home in Florida? I assume since I own a business, that I also have my own home. She hesitated a beat before continuing, "And I'm also wondering why my aunt isn't here, since I've been so sick."

Symphony saw Alex freeze in the middle of putting away some of her things, though she was not prepared for the shock and sadness that crossed the woman's features.

"What is it?" she asked her. "Just tell me the truth. It's the only way that I'll begin to put the pieces back together."

Alex nodded and sat on the edge of the bed next to Symphony. Carla Faye walked in and removed the tray. She'd only smiled when she picked it up, still nearly full.

Alex smoothed out an imaginary wrinkle in the comforter and took a deep breath before she spoke. "Hasn't Terry talked to you about any of this?"

"No, there never was a chance. I've not gotten a good explanation from anyone about anything. There's just been one thing after another. I figured, since I'm here and we're friends, then *you* know everything." She paused a moment, unsure if she should mention it, but felt it couldn't hurt. "I dreamed of a guy last night, and it wasn't Terry." She leaned in and whispered, though they were the only two in the room, "A white man."

Symphony was expecting to see surprise in Alex's eyes, but when she didn't, she knew that the man in the pictures and in her dreams was important to her story.

"Kyle Dean," Alex stated flatly.

"Yes, that's the name I saw in my phone."

"Are you sure you're ready for this, Symphony?"

"No, but I need to know what's going on."

Alex smiled at that, and Symphony felt confident that she was finally about to get some truth—whether she wanted it or not.

"Your aunt isn't here, Symphony, because she passed away."

Deep down, Symphony had known but had not wanted to accept it. She was just hoping the grief she was feeling was somehow tied to finding out about the baby.

Alex studied her. "You ok?"

"She had cancer, didn't she?"

"Yes. You remember that?"

"Not exactly. It doesn't feel quite like trying to remember a phone number or a face, it's like just remembering that you have to scratch the surface of a memory in order to recall knowing about it… I know it sounds weird, but everything seems like it's just right there. Like an orgasm that you can't quite reach." She giggled.

They both laughed out loud—long and hard. Or as hard as Symphony could with a stitched belly.

"You know what's weird, Alex?"

"What?"

"There're no pictures of Terry in my phone, nor is he listed in my contacts."

"Symphony, you've been staying at my home in Baton Rouge because you didn't want anyone to know where you were, especially Terry Phoenix and Kyle Dean."

"Why?"

So, Alex told her.

And after the telling, Symphony asked, "So I hadn't been dating or had even seen Terry until my aunt's funeral?"

"Yes."

"And I'd just met Kyle, on the way to my aunt's funeral?"

"Yes."

"…and had been with him up until I discovered he had a wife in New Orleans?"

"Yes."

"So, the baby?"

"Kyle's," Alex affirmed.

"The guy in my phone and who I'd been dreaming about?"

"Yes."

"Was I in love with him?"

"Yes."

"I was in love with a man who had a wife hidden in New Orleans where we were going away for the first time."

"Yes, but Symphony, there has to be a story there. You should've seen his face. He was just as shocked as all of us when she walked up."

"I bet he was."

"Symphony, you can't keep shutting people out when you *think* they've stepped out of bounds of your imaginary lines."

What was Alex talking about? Did she do that? Her recent memories were fuzzy and just out of grasp, but she clearly remembered how her parents chose drugs and whatever else over her. She also remembered the feeling that if her own parents couldn't be trusted to love her, how could anyone else?

"That's ridiculous," she said, shaking her head back and forth.

"Is it, Symphony?" Alex stood. Symphony could tell she was about to get a good tongue-lashing about how wrong she was.

Symphony smiled and shook her head. "Sit down, Alex. I'm not finished." Alex sat her tiny frame back on the bed with a little reluctance, but her eyebrow was cocked—just waiting to check Symphony.

"Oh yes. We are friends."

Alex's features softened. "Yes, we were fast friends."

"What I was going to say, before I was so rudely interrupted, was I can't believe I thought that way." Alex lifted both brows then. "Maybe, I needed the amnesia to get a new mindset."

"Maybe."

Symphony looked around the beautifully decorated room in different tones of gray and silver and noticed, for the first time, the packages sitting against the wall by the closet. Alex followed her eyes.

"Those were from the baby shower. We hadn't gotten around to shipping them to Florida yet."

"I don't think I could stand to see them in my home."

Alex walked over to the pile. "I know it's a lot, but it's stuff you'll need, eventually." Symphony watched Alex pick up a pink ruffled dress. "Isn't this the most precious thing?"

The sadness of never knowing her daughter took her breath away. She tried to steady herself and keep the tears from falling, but it was useless.

Alex looked toward Symphony then.

"What's wrong?"

"I never got a chance to hold her."

"I know, but…" Symphony saw Alex through the unfocused wrinkle of her tears.

Alex looked confused. Her breath hitched, and she placed a hand over her mouth. "Oh God, Symphony. You think you lost her?" she asked. "You think you lost her." A statement that time.

Symphony sat up, confused. A tiny rattle of hope unfurled like a butterfly releasing from the cocoon. She sniffed loudly. "The doctor said—"

"Symphony, you didn't lose the baby."

Confusion made her frown.

"I didn't?"

"No, sweetie. You had a big, bouncing baby girl."

Alex reached for a tissue on the nightstand and held it out to Symphony, but she didn't reach for it.

"I did."

"You did!"

Symphony paid no attention to Alex cleaning up her face. Her mind was whirling. *I didn't lose the baby. I didn't lose the baby.* She grabbled Alex's hands. "My daughter is alive?"

"Alive and well."

Symphony covered her face with her own hands and sobbed. There was a tightening in her belly, but she didn't care. Her baby was alive!

She cried for a while—until her hands were wet with tears and snot. When she uncovered her face, she saw Alex's eyes were filled with tears as well. Symphony reached for a tissue and stopped, mid-reach.

"What's wrong?" Alex asked her. She grabbed her own tissue.

"The papers. There were papers here." She looked at Alex. "You created documents for me…in case," she hesitated, "in case something went wrong."

"Yes," Alex said gently. "But everything is ok now."

"Where is she?"

"Cadence is with Kyle's family in Florida."

"Cadence? That's her name?"

"Yes, her name is Cadence—"

"Alexandra Dean." Symphony finished her daughter's name for Alex.

"Yes! You remember?"

"I guess so." While Symphony was wondering how the last bits of information had sprung out of her memory, a question came to mind. "Why does Kyle's parents have her and not Kyle?"

Alex told Symphony what Kyle's parents had told her about his mission and not being able to contact him while he was away.

Symphony wondered what kind of danger he was in and when he would be back. What was the deal with the wife that had come out of nowhere? She suddenly had to know. She wanted there to be a good explanation.

Did that mean she still had feelings for Kyle? There were so many questions swirling around in her mind. She also wondered what to do with Terry. They hadn't been together recently, but when she awoke from the coma, she'd remembered being in love with him. Was their love so strong after all this time?

Two men who loved her, so it seemed.

No wonder she'd lost her memory.

Chapter Twelve

"Why did the people at the hospital think you were my fiancé?"

Symphony was sitting up in bed watching what looked to be a chick flick he'd seen advertised before. The moment the words came out of her mouth, he knew the jig was up. They hadn't had a real conversation since she'd awaken from the coma, but Terry knew that they were about to have one now.

Did she finally remember? If she did, Terry didn't know if it was a good thing or not.

He'd missed her being discharged from the hospital. Alexandra sent Joshua a text letting them know that she would be bringing Symphony back to her house. Joshua had refused to let him leave the office because the deal he'd been working on was about to fall through. It was a deal the company couldn't afford to lose.

"I didn't tell them that. The nurse I initially met told them I was your fiancé, so I could see you."

"So, you took advantage of my fucked up brain so you could see me, when you knew I wanted the exact opposite?"

There was that foul mouth she'd somehow developed since college. He knew then that Symphony regaining her memory was a good thing for her, but definitely not for him.

"Symphony, I would have lied to Mother Theresa or anyone else in order to see you." He was honest with her. His heart thundered in his chest. What would she say or do now that she knew the truth? "You were in a coma for Christ's sake. I *needed* to see you." He looked down at the planks in the wood floor and paused for more than a few seconds. He looked up at her. "I thought I was going to lose you." His voice was desperate, but he hoped the volume in his gaze spoke for him. "I didn't know if I would ever get to see you again."

Terry hadn't moved from just inside of the doorway. He wasn't sure if he should move forward or backward. Symphony gave away nothing of how she was feeling. She just stared at him. "Say something," he pleaded.

"I'm sorry," she said, quietly.

He watched a shield of sadness cover her face when she lowered her eyes.

His heart pushed him forward, and he knelt next to the bed, placing both of his hands on hers. "Baby, what's wrong?" He felt her stiffen.

"Terry…"

"Ok… I know. It's just so hard not to call you that. I've been loving you for so long."

She used the other hand to pinch the bridge of her nose and shook her head. "No, I mean…I'm sorry for pushing you away."

That was not what he was expecting her to say. What did she mean? For pushing him away? Which time? Hope wanted to take bloom in his heart, but he was wary of that dirty little bastard. And what about the baby?

"Have you gotten your memory back?" He had to know.

"I've been getting flashes, but Alex and I had a long talk." She sucked in a long breath. "I found out about my aunt."

He wished he would have been there. He hated that she'd had to relive that event. It must've been painful. He knew how much she'd loved the woman who raised her. "I'm sorry I wasn't at the hospital when you were released."

"Alex told me you had urgent business."

"Yeah, I've kinda been neglecting things lately."

"To find me?"

"Yes."

"Here I am."

"Yes."

"Now what?"

"Now we get you well and keep you safe."

Symphony's forehead creased. Surely, she hadn't forgotten about the incident at the hospital. Some maniac had her name and picture in his pocket.

"I've already called Detective Sanchez about extra patrols in this area."

"Why?"

"Symphony! Some ex-con had your name and picture in his wallet. What do you think he was doing, looking to deliver you flowers?" He felt her stiffen. His words were harsher than he had intended them to be.

"I don't know what he was doing, but why do we have to jump to conclusions?"

"Because I don't have a conclusion. That means I need to jump to one!"

He really hadn't meant for the conversation to take a turn in this direction. He wanted to get back to what she meant about being sorry.

"Let's table that discussion for another time."

"Why do we need to have that discussion at all?"

He took a deep breath without trying to look like he needed to calm down.

"Symphony, what did you mean when you said you were sorry for pushing me away?" He watched her settle back against the headboard, as if this was a safer subject. He guessed that it was a good thing that she appeared to relax a bit.

God, she was beautiful. Her face always held just a hint of melancholy. It was part of her beauty, and it made him want to hold her. It had been so long since he really held her, but he was sure it was too soon for all of that. She still hadn't answered him. "Symphony?"

"I know I pushed you away in college. I was too scared to trust someone with my heart. So, I did what I always do when I get too close to someone— too dependent on how they make me feel. I push them away, so I don't risk being disappointed by them. It was too hard to risk my feelings getting intertwined with someone else's." She pulled her hand free and waved her hands around. "You know how vines do…they are so intertwined with others that you don't know where one starts and ends."

That sounded perfect to Terry. That's exactly what he'd wanted between the two of them.

"I'm no expert, but I'm thinking that's how it's supposed to be," he said.

She frowned. "Maybe, but I was afraid of what would happen if one of the vines pulled away. I would be left unsupported, emotionally and…" she hesitated, "vulnerable…unable to climb on my own."

Terry stood, rubbing his knees. "I've got to get off this floor. My knees are killing me. May I?" He gestured to the bed. She nodded.

At the time, he hadn't known why she'd pushed him away, but over the years, and after he'd gotten over his hurt feelings, he wondered if her decision to break things off had anything to do with her parents. That was when he decided to get her back.

"What about now?" he asked, taking possession of her hand again. "Symphony, what about now?" he asked again, needing an answer. "I've never stopped loving you. Never!" He wanted her to believe it—wanted her to know she would not have to worry about being hurt or scared or abandoned as long as he had breath in his body. As long as he had blood pumping in his heart, all her worries would become his. "Are you willing to let me love you again? I promise you will never have to worry about your heart when it's in my care."

Maybe it was too soon to ask.

Maybe it wasn't, but he wanted to know how she felt. He wanted her to know where he stood. And he wanted to stand wherever she was—holding her, shielding her, protecting her.

Oh, how he wanted this beautiful, talented, and yes, fucked up woman. Terry knew she was flawed, knew she was fighting demons, and knew the road ahead would be rocky as hell. But he was willing… so willing, to risk his own heart to have her. In the end, he was positive it would be worth it.

"So, what do you say, Symphony? Are you finally ready to give me your heart for safekeeping?"

"How can she possibly do that when she's already given it to me?" The voice came from the doorway.

What. The. Hell.

This guy was like a damn gnat!

Terry stood to face the nuisance—or more aptly, his nemesis.

"What the hell are you doing here, Dean?"

Chapter Thirteen

The sun bloomed under her skin.

It was the face, the smile, the hair, the voice, the everything from her dreams.

It was Kyle.

He was real.

He was not just something from her dreams—something her mind had conjured in all of its brokenness. He was not just some story that Alex had told her. He was real.

He was *really* real.

And if *he* was real…

Could she really have a baby?

She had the scar. She'd seen the gifts and now the man, but did she really have a daughter? She wanted to see her, breathe her in, hold her. She already loved her. She fell in love with her when she'd found out that she'd had a baby.

"I'm here to see the woman I love and the mother of my child. The question is, what are you doing her, Phoenix?"

"Where is she?" The words rushed out of her mouth before Terry had an opportunity to answer the question. She barely noticed that he was standing casually—possessively—next to the bed with both hands in his pockets.

"She's on her way," he said softly. "My parents didn't want to fly with her since she's so young. Too many germs in airports and on planes. They are driving here."

"How did *you* get here?" she asked.

"I flew."

"From?"

"Out of Orlando."

"So, you're back?"

"Yes."

Symphony's eyes were trained on Kyle, but she could feel Terry looking at her.

"And she's ok?"

"She's perfect." Her throat tightened, and the backs of her eyes stung. "Would you like to see a picture of her?"

"Wh—what?"

"I have a picture or two, or a thousand." He grinned, pulling his phone from his pocket. His grin was infectious. She returned it. "Phoenix, do you mind giving us some privacy? There are some things Symphony and I need to discuss."

Terry looked like he wanted to do no such thing. "Symphony?" Terry asked. She could see the pulse ticking in his jaw and knew he wasn't happy about being interrupted, but Kyle was the father of her child, and yes, they absolutely needed to speak privately. Plus, she couldn't wait to see what their daughter looked like.

"I think it's best."

Terry acquiesced after moment. "Sure," he said to Symphony, "if that's what you want. He walked toward the door, paused at where Kyle stood, and turned back to her. "I'll be back shortly. I have a few phone calls to make." He faced Kyle "She's been through a lot. She doesn't need anything else to upset her." Kyle lifted his chin. They stood there squaring off like this was the Wild West, for Pete's sake, before Terry turned and walked away.

Symphony did her best to avoid rolling her eyes. She did, however, look at the two handsome men and wondered what in the world she was going to do. No wonder she'd been hidden out for months. This was a complete and utter mess!

After the first picture, the rest were blurs. She was so beautiful. Symphony didn't know she could love another human so much, so quickly. Her heart ached, and her tears fell unchecked. Kyle gathered her in his arms, and she went willingly. Flashes of her grief from her aunt's funeral surfaced. The feeling of him holding her, caring for her, and making her feel safe was rushing back to her in waves of recognition. She knew these arms, this feeling, and this man.

"You're so beautiful," he whispered against her hair. "You have no idea how much I've missed you."

She knew that was a lie. She'd been in the hospital for over a week and had seen her reflection in the mirror. Her usually reddish-bronze locks were a flat, brown, frizzy disaster. Alex tried taming it to no avail. Had he really missed her? Her conversation with Alex came back to her.

He had a wife.

"You are a liar." She pushed away from him. His liquid blue eyes were hurt. The pain in them made her look away. She felt uneasy. Had the accusation been too harsh? His reaction let her know that she wasn't referring to his comment about her beauty.

"I've never lied to you, Symphony."

She grabbed a tissue and wiped her face. "I assume you've talked to Alex, and she's told you that I've been struggling with my memory."

"Yes."

"There are lots of blank spaces in my head, but I do distinctly remember you telling me you had a wife." That memory had come to her when she'd taken a nap after her conversation with Alex. "So, are you telling me that isn't true? That you didn't tell me you had a wife."

"That's not what I'm saying, Symphony."

"What are you saying, Kyle?"

He rubbed his fingers through his hair. She noticed he needed a haircut and a shave. The dark blond shadow on his face made him appear exotic and rugged. She wanted to reach up and feel it.

"I'm saying, yes, I did tell you I had a wife, but I didn't lie to you."

"So, I'm to believe that you spending time with me for all those months, in my shop, on the beach, and in my bed was not supposed to indicate that we were in an exclusive relationship?" Before he could answer, her eyes widened, and she took in a loud sharp breath.

"Baby, what's wrong? Are you hurt?" She vaguely noticed that Terry used the same endearment only a few minutes before.

He reached for her, and she steadied herself by holding on to his arm. Just like that, everything from her being annoyed at the airport, him showing up at her aunt's service, the times they'd made love in her office, his car, her home, his studio, and all the other times they'd spent just being together had come back to her. It was like a million puzzle pieces flying into her head and fitting themselves together. "I remember." She looked up at him, stunned. "I remember everything, Kyle."

She felt almost complete. Her mind felt clear. The sound that escaped her was part cry and part laughter. Kyle cupped her face—the excitement of her memory recovery was evident in the way his entire face smiled.

Every time he touched her, she felt it. A hot pulsing, electrifying jolt. His touch was also comforting and safe, yet exciting.

She could see it coming. She knew his intentions. She wanted to stop it, wanted to not want it, but she did want it. She needed the kiss that she knew was coming. She wanted to soak it up like the desert absorbed rain.

His kisses, she remembered clearly. And when he captured her mouth to kiss her, her soul drank it in.

At the end of it, Symphony's lids were heavy, and her chest rose and fell in pace with the quick beats of her heart.

His kiss.

She'd pulled away first and leaned back against the headboard to steady her world. It was currently spinning off its axis for more than one reason.

Goodness!

Kyle's kiss tasted like a long-awaited vacation. Though somewhere in her newly unjumbled mind, Symphony couldn't help but wonder if Terry's kisses would taste like home.

Chapter Fourteen

Kyle poured his entire being into that kiss. His love, his soul, his heart, himself. He loved this woman. He wanted her back in his life. He needed her. He had to make her understand that they belonged together. From the first moment they'd met, he was hooked like a junkie on heroin.

There's no way she could deny their attraction to one another. Even more than that, she couldn't deny the love they had for one another. It hadn't taken her long to remember him. She just had to be reminded of their connection.

Kyle watched her trying to gain control of herself after their kiss. He didn't want to ruin the moment, but he had to clear the air about Shelia.

"Symphony, I want to talk about that day in New Orleans."

"You mean when you told me you had a wife?"

Her words were sharp, and he felt them like a physical blow. "Yes." She was about to say something else, but he stopped her. "I'm sorry Symphony, but I need you to listen to me." Her head tilted in that way he loved. It was when he knew she wanted to cuss but was giving him the benefit of the doubt first. "You didn't give me a chance then, and I've been in hell since, because you hadn't given me the opportunity to explain to you the circumstance of the marriage."

Her chin lifted, and her entire face closed off to him as she turned away. "So, I didn't hear you wrong? I wasn't mistaken? You're married?" She slid her leg away from him, like she was already trying to distance herself.

He had to make her understand. Had to make her believe that the only connection he'd had with Shelia was because of a sense of obligation.

"Is that why you didn't tell me about the baby?" The words coming out harsher than he'd intended. Or maybe he did intend for them to hurt her—to sting just a little. "I was going through hell trying to find you, so I could explain that I'd only married Shelia, the sister of my childhood friend, to give her health insurance because she'd once practically saved my life." She looked at him then. "And here you were hiding away a secret of your own." A flash in her eyes, told him he'd hit his mark that time.

Things had happened so quickly when he'd returned home that he hadn't had a chance to process what Symphony had done. She'd purposely withheld from him the knowledge that he would be a father.

"Did you only contact me because you were worried—" He was going to say, *you might die*, but couldn't make himself say the words, because he *did* almost lose her. "Because you were worried things wouldn't go well?"

The guilt that played in her eyes told him he'd hit the nail on the head. The realization that he may not have ever known he was a father pushed him to his feet. He was the one who now needed distance from her.

"Damn it, Symphony!" he accused, backing away from her. "Do you know how monumentally fucked up that is?"

"Do you know how fucked up it is, to finally realize that you can love again after being hurt so many times, and then to find out that man has a *wife*?" Her words were slow and controlled, but pain punctuated every syllable.

It was not his intention to fight with her, but to know that he might not ever have known his precious little girl left him weak. He turned from her, placed his hands on his head, and took a deep breath. He refused to be consumed by the what ifs.

Wait.

What did she say?

Did she say, she—

Loved him?

He faced her, and he saw that determined chin of hers lift again. "Did you just say you—"

"You have to understand, Kyle." She cut him off. Her voice on the verge of pleading. "I was in very unfamiliar territory."

"When did you find out you were pregnant?"

"Something Alex said to me that day in the lobby made me realize that I hadn't had a period in a couple months. Just when that whirlwind damn near knocked me to my knees, Shelia sauntered up, and… well…you know what happened next."

For a long while, their eyes held, the space between them filled with emotions too complex to acknowledge. The moment was fragile, and they both knew it.

"I died a little every day when I couldn't find you. Symphony, I loved you then, and I love you now." He watched her eyes slide close. "I've loved you from the moment I saw that box of pastries in your hand."

"You just wanted inside my box." Her smile was playful, but her eyes were serious.

"I wanted inside your heart." He walked forward, stopping next to the bed, and sat. The first time I saw you smile, you lit something within me. And since you'd given me such a hard time before I got one of those lovely smiles, I knew it wasn't something you gave away freely." He reached for her hand. "I didn't know you, but I wanted to be the one who could bring you from a place that lacked joy, to a place where you wouldn't remember a time when you didn't have it.

"Baby, I'm sorry I hurt you. I'm sorry that I became something you wanted to run from." He shook his head, berating himself. "I should have taken care of detaching myself from Shelia long ago. The missions when I was in the Army and well…frankly, I didn't have plans on being in an exclusive relationship where my marital status would matter." Her eyes lowered first, then her head. He lifted her chin with his index finger, wanting her to look at him. He wanted her to see the sincerity in his eyes. "Until I met you," he said.

"Symphony, you were a stranger to me, but I had to be at your aunt's funeral for you. I felt like we'd made a connection, and I wanted to be there. I wanted to be the one who held you through your grief. So, I showed up, even though I was risking being thrown out on my ass. I showed up on the slight chance you'd let me stay."

He felt her hand tremble and saw the tear slip free from her lashes. "That all seems like a lifetime ago." Her words were barely a whisper.

"It was," he said plainly. "This is a new chapter. We have a new life that we created together." She smiled at the mentioning of their daughter. "And Shelia is no longer in the picture." It still saddened him that she was dead, but he tried not to show it. He didn't want Symphony to get the wrong idea.

"You got a divorce?"

"It's the reason I took the photography job. It was either do that or lose the shop."

"What do you mean?"

He described briefly how Shelia was trying to extort money out of him and why he felt the need to marry her in the first place. "It was the drugs and all the other shit she was into. The Shelia you saw is not the girl I grew up with."

"You had to pay her off?" she asked, stunned. "You were willing to lose the studio to divorce her?"

"I was willing to do just about anything to get you back, and Shelia was an obstacle in my way. I endured some potentially life-altering atrocities for a chance to get back in your life."

"So, you're divorced now?"

"Technically, I'm widowed." Symphony's eyes grew wide. "Yes, I was shocked to find out she'd been found dead while I was away."

Kyle could tell Symphony wanted to ask more questions, but it wasn't something he wanted to discuss. At least not right now. He gently squeezed her fingers. "I'm hoping the mistakes of my youth will not keep me from my future." She was about to say something when Kyle placed a finger on her lips to silence her. The kiss that followed filled him with hope that his future could be starting right now.

At the end of the kiss, Kyle pressed his forehead against hers. When he could form a coherent thought again, he whispered against her lips, "You're my future, Symphony…you and Cadence. I promise I will spend my life chasing sadness away from the two of you."

***

Terry walked up to the cracked door at the end of their kiss and heard Kyle's promise. *How the hell is this happening again?* he thought. It had to have meant something that even when she'd lost her memory, she'd never forgotten him. He just had to find a way to prove it to her. With the baby coming and Kyle underfoot, it would be difficult, but he believed in fate. Symphony was his fate.

Chapter Fifteen

"Shouldn't they be here by now?" Symphony asked Kyle. They were all sitting in the large living room waiting for Kyle's parents to arrive with the baby. Alex sat next to her on one of the oversized sofas with some ideas she'd written out of how Symphony could expand without losing the quality of her pastries, which is why she'd refused to sell out to the frozen food corporation.

Kyle and Joshua were on the other sofa, talking about the many refugees being denied entrance to too many countries, and Terry sat in a chair working on his laptop, though Symphony could tell he was distracted. If anyone saw the looks he kept giving Kyle and then her, they didn't comment on it.

The waiting filled her with anxiety and having everyone in one room was downright awkward.

Kyle broke away from the conversation with Joshua to look at his watch and the wall clock above the fireplace mantle. "Yes, I was expecting them a couple hours ago. They are driving the RV, but maybe they had to stop more often with the baby."

"Call and see where they are."

"I did, both their phones went to voicemail." Kyle picked up his phone again and placed another call.

Symphony no longer tried to hide her disappointment when Kyle clicked off the phone and shook his head at her. Worry was starting to eat away at her stomach.

"When's the last time you heard from them, Kyle?" It was Joshua who asked.

"I haven't talked to them since breakfast, which was about six hours ago." He looked through his phone again. "Oh wait…here's a text saying they're thirty minutes out."

Excitement and nervousness took root in Symphony again.

"Hmm…I guess I didn't hear the phone go off. That text came in about two hours ago."

Everyone looked up at him.

"Even with Baton Rouge traffic, they should be here by now," Alex stated.

The doorbell rang, and everyone relaxed again. Alex and Kyle went to the door. Symphony was too nervous and emotional to move. She turned to look at the door expectantly. Alex opened it, looked around, and Kyle bent down to pick up an envelope. "Oh, it was just a courier dropping off some mail."

"That must be the contracts I'm waiting on," Terry said, standing to retrieve the envelope.

"No," Kyle said. "It's addressed to Symphony."

Kyle handed the package to Symphony. She was puzzled. She wasn't expecting anything, but maybe her mind hadn't quite filled in all the chinks.

"Who's it from, Symphony?" Terry asked.

Symphony saw Kyle level an eye at Terry, as if he thought he was being a bit nosey. She looked at the envelope. "I don't know. There's no return address." She looked up at Terry. She was sure his mind was where hers was going, though she'd all but forgotten about the man at the hospital.

"Give it here."

"I'm sure Symphony is capable of—"

"Stay out of this, Dean."

Symphony handed Terry the envelope. "You don't think it's…" Her voice trailed off.

He took the envelope and shook it gently. Then he felt around it. He walked to the kitchen and placed it on the counter. By this time, Joshua had followed him in there. Terry opened the envelope carefully and extracted a single sheet of paper and then dropped it on the counter, as if he didn't want to touch it anymore. He turned to Joshua and then he looked toward Symphony.

Something was wrong. She knew it.

"The baby?"

"Josh," Terry gestured for Joshua to look at the paper. Terry pulled a card from his wallet and picked up the handset on the wall to dial the number on the card. Joshua read the words aloud.

"You will soon know how it feels to want something and not get it."

Kyle looked at Symphony. "What about the baby?" He turned to the men in the kitchen. "Will someone please tell me what the hell is going on?"

When Terry got off the phone with Detective Sanchez, he explained to Kyle what was going on. He told him about the shooting at the hospital and the death of the man who had Symphony's name and picture in his pocket.

"What does this have to do with that letter?" she heard Kyle ask. Symphony was busy trying to keep herself from tipping over into lunacy.

"We don't know, but I'm afraid that it may have something to do with why your parents haven't arrived."

"Wait…what? You think this lunatic who sent this note may have taken my family?"

"I hope not, Kyle, but it's too much of a coincidence to ignore the possibility," Terry stated.

126

Within fifteen minutes of Detective Sanchez's arrival, the house was swarming with police officers and other detectives. On the way to the house, Detective Sanchez had already put in a call to state troopers. They'd found the RV parked at a rest area near Lafayette. There was no one in it, but the keys were still in the ignition.

Someone must have called her back to the house, because Symphony was sure Carla Faye had already gone for the evening. Symphony was vaguely aware that the woman was busy in the kitchen and preparing sandwiches, iced tea, and coffee for anyone who wanted them. She was sure Mrs. Briggs hadn't hesitated to return. She constantly wished aloud that Alex and Joshua lived in Baton Rouge full-time, to give her more to do than sit at home with her husband, Oscar. Tonight, she got her wish, because she seemed to have lots to do.

Carla Faye was in her seventies but had the spirit and physical ability of a much younger woman. Symphony had not met Oscar, but she hoped the man had the stamina to be able to keep up with his wife. The long-time housekeeper moved about the kitchen and living room so unobtrusively that Symphony wondered how many times she'd done it in the past and what secrets she gleaned. Symphony admired her loyalty to the family.

Watching Carla Faye made Symphony think of Aunt Helen, who was a lot like Carla Faye. Aunt Helen loved to serve others. More specifically, she loved to serve them good desserts. Some people saw her only as the lady who owned a bakery, but she was so much more than that. She was such an incredible business woman that she invested well, so well that when she died, she was quite wealthy. She did what she loved until she didn't want to do it anymore, and then she retired on a semi-private island and did anything she pleased.

"Have something to eat, Ms. Symphony. You're going to need your strength for when the baby comes home." She handed Symphony a small plate with half of a ham sandwich. "Newborns are a joy, but as small as they are, they are very demanding. Just wait, you'll see." She smiled sweetly, but her eyes shown with every bit of confidence to support the words she'd just spoken. Symphony wanted so desperately to believe her. She wanted to believe that her baby would be found and brought home to her.

She took a bite of the sandwich, not tasting a thing, but she didn't want Carla Faye to worry about her. "That's it. Eat up, honey. I'll get you some iced tea to wash that down." When she walked off, Symphony ate the rest of the sandwich and had to admit that she did feel a tiny bit better physically, but emotionally, she was still a mess. She would be until her baby was brought to her and safely placed in her arms.

When Carla Faye finally convinced Alex and Joshua to come to the kitchen for a bite, Symphony was left to watch Kyle pace back and forth while one of the detectives asked questions that must not have made any sense to him, because he kept looking at the man like he'd lost his mind. She was having her own difficult time with the questions.

No, she could not think of anyone who would want to harm her. At this point, it was certain she was the target. Of what? She didn't know.

"What about past boyfriends? Love interests gone bad?" The detective prodded.

"I've been in love twice in my life, and both of them are right in this room."

The detective looked around, and both Kyle and Terry were staring at Symphony. "I've met Terry Phoenix. And you say Kyle is the father of your daughter?" He looked at her, pointedly and then back at Kyle and Terry. "Maybe we should continue this conversation in private."

"Detective Sanchez, I have nothing to hide from any of the people in this room, and I'm certain that neither Kyle Dean nor Terry Phoenix wish to see me or my daughter come to any harm. I've already explained to you why Terry introduced himself as my fiancé."

She saw Kyle's eyes narrow at Terry.

Dear Lord, this was a complete circus.

"So, these are the only two men you've dated?"

"I didn't say that. You asked about boyfriends or love interests."

"Can you tell me about other men you've dated or been involved with?"

Symphony's eyes flicked to Terry for an instant. She'd talked about her previous dalliances with other men with Kyle, but she knew that Terry would be shocked about her history with other men. She wasn't ashamed of her life, but she knew he wouldn't understand.

She told Sanchez about each man she'd been involved with, and how each affair ended, if it went beyond one night. She never thought anyone would ask about any of this. Why would anyone question her about her sex life? But here she was putting all her business out in the streets.

"What about this Eric guy?"

"Eric?"

"Yes."

"What about him?"

"You said you met with him twice a month…for how long?"

Symphony watched Terry walk out of the room. Her eyes followed him until they met up with Kyle's watchful gaze. What was he thinking about her? Whatever it was…whatever she was…all she had right now was the truth—for either of them. For anyone.

"A few months."

"How did he feel about the breakup?"

"There was no breakup. We just parted ways."

"He held no animosity toward you?"

"If he did, I wasn't aware of it."

"And you say you got a restraining order against Delton Cleveland?" He looked at her and lifted a brow, as if somehow it was her fault that the fool was crazy and cut up all her clothes.

"Yes. He was my first attempt at a relationship after Te—" She was going to say "Terry" but said, "after college," instead.

"Any others?"

"Griffin George thought we were in a relationship."

"And you?'

"I thought we were good friends with a common interest."

"Which was?"

"Classical music. Yea, no pun intended." Her aunt named her Symphony, because Aunt Helen was a lover of classical music. Symphony was exposed to it at an early age and developed a love for it as well. Most people thought she was being sarcastic when she said she loved the symphony.

He nodded his head and chuckled uncomfortably. She knew he didn't get her joke.

"This Griffin guy, he proposed marriage?"

"Yes. I was not interested. He was also insistent on me mending things with my parents."

"Your parents?"

Symphony took the time to tell him the sordid details of her childhood and how she subsequently ended up living with Aunt Helen.

He seemed to ask her endless questions when she only had one. Where the hell was her daughter and Kyle's parents?

"Have you seen or heard from your parents since you were little?"

"My mother was at the dinner when Griffin proposed, and I haven't heard from my dad since I turned him down when he asked me for money from prison."

"Your father was in prison?"

"Yes. He may still be in there. I don't know." She'd had enough. "We're wasting time with all these pointless questions. What are you going to do to find my daughter and her grandparents?"

"We're going to do all we can, Ms. James."

She wanted to scream.

Chapter Sixteen

Was he never going to get a chance to have a conversation with Symphony? What the hell, man! For months, he'd searched for her, and when he finally found her, she was in a coma. When she came out of the coma, she had no memory. When she was well enough to move from ICU, some lunatic found out his wife's baby wasn't his when the baby needed blood, decided to kill his wife, and ended up killing a man who was apparently after Symphony in the process.

And just when he was finally—finally—getting somewhere with Symphony, expressing his love, and asking her to trust him with her heart again, Kyle Beach Bum Dean decided to show up from Bumfuck, Egypt, destroying his moment.

As if today wasn't bad enough when he'd walked up to witness the woman he loved kissing another man, and that man promising to be her sadness chaser, he had to listen to Symphony tell the detective about her freak fest over the past few years.

But the real kicker…the real kicker… was all that shit paled in contrast to knowing that she now shared a child with a man who wasn't him.

A child who was now officially missing, along with the man's parents.

He needed a drink.

Terry walked back into the living room. He was man enough to admit that he'd been hiding out. He just couldn't listen to Symphony talk about hooking up with men like she was going to get an oil change.

Most of the officers were gone, but a few remained. It had looked like a scene from a movie, earlier. No movie he wanted to be in.

Terry spotted Joshua alone in the kitchen.

"Hey, Cuz, you have some of that scotch I like?" he asked, noticing Joshua already had a glass in his hand.

"Sure, man. It's in the rec room. Want me to get it, or do you want to come up and chill for a while?"

Terry looked over to Symphony and saw her talking to Kyle. "We can go up and chill."

"Should we see if Kyle wants to join us? This has to be rough on the man."

Terry inwardly rolled his eyes. That was exactly the opposite of what he wanted to do, but he mumbled, "Whatever, man."

Joshua asked Kyle if he wanted something to drink. He hesitated for just a moment when he saw Terry with him but got up anyway.

Yeah, I'm still here. Terry thought to himself. *As long as Symphony is here, I'm making Baton Rouge, Louisiana my home too.*

He wasn't feeling generous and had no plans on just handing his woman over to this guy.

The rec room was essentially Joshua's man cave. It was decked out with all the amenities a man could need: flat screen television, pool table, well-stocked bar, full-sized fridge, and poker table. Of course, it also had all the upscale lounging furniture a man could hope for. However, at the moment, all Terry worried about was the bar, and more specifically, the scotch.

After they were all settled with a glass in hand, an awkward silence hung heavily around them.

"So, Kyle, the last time we saw each other, you had a wife step out into the wings." It was Joshua who'd started this thread of conversation, and Terry was glad he didn't have to, because he damn sure wanted to know what the pretty boy was hiding. He leaned in, waiting on Dean's answer.

Kyle took a moment to look at both men before he answered. "Honestly, Joshua, my initial answer would be that it's none of your damn business, and that it's between me and Symphony."

"But you've decided to amend that, right?" Joshua calmly retorted.

"Yes, because if it weren't for you and your wife, my daughter and Symphony may not be here." Terry had to hand it to Dean, Joshua could be pretty damn intimidating at times, but he wasn't ruffled at all.

"Well?" Joshua pressed. "Is she your wife?"

"Shelia. Her name is Shelia, and she's dead." Neither man was expecting that. "And yes, she was my wife."

The admission filled Terry with both smugness at being correct in not trusting him and ire that the dude had the audacity to try and two-time, Symphony.

"And you thought it was cool to have a wife and…see Symphony?" Terry asked him. He was going to say, "date Symphony," but couldn't bring himself to say the words. He took a long swig from his glass. The golden liquid burned going down and it felt good.

Kyle looked from one man to the other. "I know what the two of you may think of me. Again, I owe no one an explanation except Symphony, but since you've asked—and frankly, I have nothing to hide—I'll tell you."

So he did.

He told them the reasons he married Shelia and why no one could contact him when Cadence was born.

"And you went through all of that because you love her that much?" Terry asked Kyle.

"Yes."

"So do I," he returned flatly.

They eyed each other for a long while, both men taking measure of the other. Kyle raised a brow and then his glass and gave a nod to Terry. The two clinked glasses. It was the equivalent to saying, "May the best man win." Terry was going to make damn sure it was him. He knew the obstacles in front of him, but he was going to give it the best shot he had.

Terry heard Joshua's quiet chuckle as he sat and watched.

***

Kyle knew that this moment with Terry was important. He was no longer an abstract figure—some guy that Symphony was involved with. He'd shared his story, and once that happened, he could no longer be just someone who was in the way.

He was a real live threat.

Chapter Seventeen

"Are you ok, Symphony?"

How could she possibly be ok?

"I don't know what I am, Alex. I'm just numb." There was a sharp ache in her chest that made it difficult to breathe. She pressed a hand against it.

"They'll find them. Are you in pain?" Symphony just looked at her. "Never mind." Alex must have realized that yes, she was in the worst pain possible. Her newborn was missing, and she'd yet to hold her in her arms.

"I feel like all of this," she waved her hands around, "feels like a very bad dream. Sometimes, I wonder if I'm still in the coma and all of the madness is just a product of the medication or my past fears coming back to haunt me." Symphony closed her eyes and shook her head. "This is some made-for-TV shit!"

"Agreed," her friend said. She loved Alex. She never sugarcoated anything or pretended things would be fine when they wouldn't. "I wonder what the guys are up to?"

Symphony made a face. "They're either all sitting up there singing 'Kumbaya,' or Joshua is watching Kyle and Terry have a dick-measuring contest."

Despite the seriousness of the situation, they both laughed. It felt good to not think for a moment. They laughed until a heavy silence fell over them, pushing them both back into their own thoughts.

Alex must have thought it better if the police went outside for a little while, because she asked them to move to the back porch. The radios with their incessant talking was nerve wracking.

"Do you think it could be someone from your past?" Alex asked quietly.

Symphony wondered about that herself. It was very difficult to think that she could have been involved with anyone who was so heartless that they would put a newborn in danger. Her parents had enough heart to not fight when Aunt Helen was given custody. The detective asked her if she knew of anyone who would want to hurt her. Of course she did.

In fact, there were lots of people it could be, if she was really being honest with herself. If they were trying to hurt her personally, that meant that Kyle's parents were just caught up in whatever twisted game this person was trying to play. And this was a very vile and twisted game.

Symphony tried to detach herself from this sick reality she was left with, because if she allowed her heart and mind to climb the steps of this particular reality, she was afraid she would slip into a madness from which she would not be able to return.

Breathe, Symphony, just breathe, she repeated over and over in her head. She had to remain calm and try not to panic. But the more time that ticked away, the more difficult remaining calm became.

Who wanted to hurt her so badly they would put a baby in jeopardy? The only way she could get to the bottom of that question was to figure out who *she'd* hurt. Who had she left so scarred and broken?

"Symphony?" Alex prodded. "It's ok if you don't want to talk about it."

She was so wrapped up in her own thoughts that she had forgotten Alex asked her a question.

"I was such a bitch, you know." Her statement strutted out of her mouth without shame or remorse. She'd never been reluctant to own the truth. Others were the ones who could never handle it. It didn't matter what people said, they wanted to be lied to. They wanted words that made them feel good, feel pretty, feel accepted, feel wanted, and well, Symphony just really didn't give a royal damn about words dressed in costume.

141

Alex's forehead creased, and her head shook slightly. "I just can't imagine you being a bitch."

"Well, I was," she stated. "I may still be. It's a title you either give yourself or others thrust upon you when you're truthful to a fault."

"People can be truthful without being bitches."

"Sure, but those people usually use words with rounded corners. My words, though not mean, are jagged and pointy most of the time."

Symphony watched Alex think about that statement. Alex's words weren't usually dipped in sugar either.

"In your gut, do you have an idea who may want to hurt you?" Symphony could tell her friend was going into attorney mode. "I'm thinking it's someone you hurt, whether intentional or not."

"I was just thinking the same thing," Symphony confessed. "The problem is, sometimes you can hurt someone and not know it." Symphony wondered if her parents knew how their lack of care had truly hurt her. "And sometimes you know and don't care."

"True," Alex agreed softly.

Symphony thought again of what Alex asked her. Was there anyone who she could have hurt?

"My dad was pretty pissed when I refused to give him money in prison." From seemingly out of thin air, Alex had a notepad in her hand, poised to take notes.

"Who else?"

"Though I'm not aware of anything in particular, I got a weird vibe from Eric when we parted."

"Why did you stop seeing him?"

"More and more often, he wanted me to stay."

"Stay where?"

"We met twice a month in a hotel room in Jacksonville. It was just sex."

"You think he wanted more?"

"Yes, I was starting to get that feeling."

"So, you ended it?"

"Yes."

"Anyone else?"

"There's the guy who cut up my clothes. I had to get a restraining order."

Alex looked up then.

"Were you in them?" she asked with all seriousness.

"No. Delton Cleveland broke into my apartment and cut up everything in my closet. And the bastard stole my favorite pair of shoes."

A single brow climbed Alex's forehead. "We'll put an asterisk by his name." She made a show of making the asterisk big and dark. "Anyone else?"

Symphony knew that many people would judge her by her past, but not Alex. Her past was just that, in the past, and Symphony loved her all the more for it.

"Griffin asked me to marry him."

"The brute!"

Symphony laughed at that. "Well, yeah!"

"Why is he a candidate?"

"He made a big show of proposing, and I ran out on him." It was that night, she realized now, that something broke inside of her. Whatever had been holding her together, from after Terry left to go back to Boston, cracked and broke away like a melting icicle falling to the pavement—shattering to pieces. Symphony realized Alex watched her quietly waiting for her to continue. "My mom was there."

Alex frowned. "Why?"

"He… Griffin, was big on family and didn't understand why I didn't want to have a relationship with my parents."

"Anyone else?"

"Cooper Read."

"That bastard," they both said in unison. Cooper Read was the man who tried to blackmail her out of her recipes. "That's all I can think of right now."

Alex tapped her pen against the pad. Symphony could see the wheels turning in her head. There were lots of notes on the pad. Symphony reached for it and began reading the list of names and paused.

"Why is my mom on this list?"

"It's a longshot, but I didn't want to rule her out."

"I've never done anything to her. Except be born, of course."

"Exactly. Her name is on the list, because you hurt her by walking out when Griffin asked you to marry him. She was part of the reason you refused him."

Symphony had never thought about her mother's reactions or feelings after she left. She didn't want to think about it now either. She took a deep breath and exhaled it in a rush. All she wanted to think about was holding her baby. And to do that, they had to figure out where she was.

Chapter Eighteen

Sleep never found Symphony during the few hours Alex demanded she try to find it. Images of Cadence flashed repeatedly in her head and left her feeling hollowed out. Logic told her that this was not her fault, but failure as a mother lurked over her and seeped into her consciousness. In addition, the battle between reason and emotion left her emotionally and physically exhausted. Not to mention the Terry and Kyle situation. It drained her as well.

Two men loved her.

She realized now that pushing Terry away was her fault. She was so afraid to lose herself in him that she never gave them a chance. She casually blamed it on them living in two different states, wanting two separate things out of life. She lived in Florida, Terry's family business was in Boston. It never occurred to her to start her business in Boston. There was no one but her aunt tying her to Florida. Helen Cole ended up going off to live in South Carolina, anyway. It was clear now that it was only fear keeping her from going forward with Terry.

So many years passed. It had to mean something that Terry was the man she'd remembered loving all those years ago.

Then there was Kyle Dean.

He'd taken her, broken and scarred, no questions asked. She'd fallen for him so quickly and so hard. Even when she'd lost her memory, his imprint in her mind never wavered. Kyle was the father of her daughter. He loved her. They could give their daughter what she'd never had—two loving parents.

Symphony didn't want to dwell on it anymore. She needed to find out who had her daughter and Kyle's parents. As for the rest, she was tired of fighting. Facing death put things in perspective. She wanted to be happy. She wanted to be loved. She wanted to love. At that moment she decided she would trust in love for the first time in her life and wondered how it would reveal itself to her.

It wasn't yet light out, but it wasn't as dark as it had been. Symphony decided it was time to get up since she couldn't sleep. She needed answers and coffee. Slipping into some decent loungewear, she headed to the kitchen.

Symphony stepped into the kitchen and stilled.

All the Phoenix men, Terry's cousins and uncle, were sitting around the table while their wives busied themselves preparing food. Everyone looked at her when she walked in.

"What're you all doing here?" Symphony asked before she could pull the words back. This was not her home.

Dixon Phoenix, who she knew was Alex's father-in-law, was an incredibly handsome man. He walked over to her and pulled her into a huge hug. What man smelled this good so early in the morning? She was stunned by her slight attraction to him, but she guessed a woman would have to be half dead not to be moved by Dixon Phoenix, no matter his age or the situation.

"Of course, we're here for you, dear," he said when he released her. "We had to come to see if we could help in some way. Helen was very special to Gloria and me. We considered her family, so that makes you family as well."

Her throat tightened. She looked around the kitchen and saw the warm smiles of all the Phoenix men—Landon, Joshua, Ethan, and all their wives. She couldn't speak if she tried. Gloria, Candice, and Sophia all rushed over to hug her as well. Symphony spotted Kyle sitting among them through her tears. She'd never been prone to tears. She could blame it on the hormones but knew they had nothing to do with them and everything to do with the people in this room.

Never in her life had she had a family like this. She was overwhelmed and under prepared for this outpouring. Her own thoughts came back to her. *How will love reveal itself to me?*

She stood there crying. Alex was the last of the ladies to hug her, but hers was the fiercest. Both Kyle and Terry stood to go to her. Both their chairs protested the backward movement. The men looked at each other, neither looking to back away, but before it became a sprint of who would get to her first, Gloria Phoenix, Dixon's wife, gave Symphony a tissue and ushered her to the open spot at the head of the table.

"Come on, dear. Sit and eat something. How are you feeling?"

"Like hell." She was honest, and Gloria patted her shoulder. She looked up at one of the officers walking in from the back porch with an empty cup in his hand. "Any news?" Symphony asked him.

All eyes were on the officer. He looked around and then back at her. "Well, ma'am, we've just got information that a vehicle was stolen from the same rest stop where the Dean's RV was abandoned."

Symphony's eyes found Kyle's.

"What took so long for you to get that information? It's been nearly ten hours since the RV was found," Alex asked.

Before the officer could answer, his cell phone rang. He answered it quickly. He looked at all the eyes staring at him and went back out to the porch. Everyone in the kitchen went back to the business of breakfast, while surreptitiously looking through the French doors separating them from the officers, who clearly had news. Symphony neither heard nor saw anything but Kyle. His gaze held hers firmly, helping her prepare for whatever was to come. She was positive that something was coming.

Someone put a plate of eggs, bacon, toast, and potatoes in front of her.

"You should eat something, Symphony." The voice was Sophia's, but Symphony didn't acknowledge her or the plate of food.

Both, Symphony and Kyle watched Landon and Ethan walk outside. They were exchanging words with the officers and then walked out of view. One of the officers followed them. Kyle looked from the doors to Symphony and pushed from the table. He went out. She couldn't move. At that moment, she realized that having people around who cared about her kept her from having to be strong all the time. She wanted to strip out of her strength like a robe and hand it over.

She was tired. Tired and defeated.

Kyle turned to her from the porch. Even through the little pane of glass, she could see the worry etched in his face. Symphony stood, the little strength she still wore sliding quietly down the length of her, pooling at her feet. She carefully stepped over it and walked out of the kitchen. "I'm sleepy," she said, without a backward glance.

Chapter Nineteen

Terry ached to go to her. He wanted to comfort Symphony when she stood to go, but he didn't attempt to. There was something in the set of her jaw that told him that anything he did would be an intrusion. Alex, too, had taken a step in Symphony's direction, but Gloria stayed her with a gentle hand on her arm. "Let her go."

Kyle walked into the kitchen. "They spotted the stolen car at the private terminal at an airport in West Houston." He looked around. "Where's Symphony?"

Terry immediately knew that's where Ethan and Landon were heading. Landon was a former international pilot, and Ethan had once owned an airfield in Australia. They still had plenty of connections in the aviation world.

Dixon pulled out his phone and punched in a number. By the conversation, he was either talking to Landon or Ethan. When he hung up, he faced Kyle. "I was going to suggest we take the company jet to Houston, but the boys are already a step ahead of us."

"Are they taking the pilot, or is Landon flying?" Alex asked him.

"Landon's flying. Why?"

"A friend of my dad has a plane on standby, in case we need it." She turned to Kyle. "I didn't tell him why I needed it. He was happy to help me, no matter the situation."

Kyle nodded.

Dixon pulled the phone out again to contact their pilot. He put Alex on the phone and she spoke to him for a little while, giving him information about the jet.

"Well, son," he said to Kyle, "let's go get your family."

Joshua was already on his feet kissing his wife and stepmother good-bye. Terry and Kyle both looked toward the only bedroom on the first floor, the guest room where Symphony was staying.

Terry wanted to go to her to assure her everything would be ok. He prayed to God they would find the baby in Houston. He watched Kyle scan the room with thankful eyes. "You have no idea how much this means to us…thank you." Terry's heart tightened when Kyle said "us." He spoke of Symphony like they were a unit.

Joshua gave Kyle a firm pat on his back. "We'll find them." They all walked to the vehicle parked out front." The agents and officers were already

153

gone. Only the men in the patrol vehicle were left out front. Terry saw the cops in the car watch them get in the SUV and drive away, but they didn't say anything to them or follow them.

From the glances Joshua kept directing at him through the rearview mirror, Terry guessed his cousin was worried about how he felt helping a man who was in love with Symphony. Terry didn't know how to assure him that was the farthest thing from his mind right now. This had nothing to do with trying to impress Symphony, but everything to do with helping a man in need. No one deserved to have their parents and child kidnapped.

Kyle was cool enough, and if the circumstances were different, he would fit in with his cousins and him perfectly. Other than this temporary truce, though, he couldn't see how that would be possible, considering everything.

What would it be like if he did get back with Symphony?

It suddenly struck Terry that he would never be rid of Kyle. He was the father of Symphony's daughter and would always be a part of their relationship. Could he handle that? Could he handle knowing Kyle was always in the wings, reminding Symphony that they could be a family?

It was at that moment that Terry decided Symphony would have to be the one to make that decision. He was sure if he continued to press her about rekindling their relationship, it would be like chasing ghosts.

Terry watched the traffic pass by the window of the SUV. When he'd first seen her in their college library all those years ago, he knew it was fate. From that moment, there wasn't a doubt in his mind that he wouldn't spend the rest of his life with Symphony.

Now, he wasn't as sure.

Now, he questioned his premonition. Was she supposed to be the woman he shared his life with, or was the premonition about something altogether different? Was he the catalyst used to make sure she got her daughter back and ended up with Kyle? He wanted that idea to seem completely ridiculous, but he knew that sometimes life taught you lessons that you never knew you needed.

When they arrived at the airport in Baton Rouge, the pilot let them know that Landon and Ethan were about thirty minutes ahead of them. All four men settled in the leather seats of the spacious cabin.

As the plane taxied out to the runway, Terry turned to Kyle and said, "Kyle, everything is going to be fine." Kyle offered a tight smile and nodded. The other two men looked relieved and nodded to Terry as well.

***

Sleep enveloped Symphony the moment her head hit the pillow. Exhaustion like she'd never experienced before allowed her to sleep. She guessed she'd been too tired to dream, because she remembered nothing but getting into bed. She didn't know how much time passed or of anything that happened outside of the bedroom since she walked in but worry snaked its way into her abdomen. Still, she would not, could not make herself get up. She didn't want to face whatever lay outside that door.

She hadn't moved in hours, but she'd been awake for some time now. Her eyes focused on the pink teddy bear sitting on the night stand. It was the only toy left among Cadence's things. The rest of the items were clothes and items Cadence would need when she got older. A hot tear burned a path to across the bridge of her nose. It tickled, but she couldn't find the strength to wipe it away. Would her daughter ever get a chance to pull the eyes out of the bear's head or snuggle with it before she drifted off to sleep?

"Symphony?" She didn't move. It was Kyle. She sucked in a deep fortifying breath. "Yes?" She didn't want to see sadness in his eyes. She didn't want to see the look of pain that would be permanently etched in her brain. She didn't want to hear him say Cadence hadn't been found.

"I have someone you've been waiting to meet."

And then she heard it—a sound better than any sonata she'd ever heard in her life. The tiny protest of a waking baby filled her ears and her soul. Symphony's throat tightened, and tears sprang from her eyes. She turned to the sound and saw Kyle standing with a beautiful buddle in his arms. She sobbed with joyous relief.

Part Two

Chapter Twenty

The music spun around her. A narrative with no words. It spoke to her soul—the parts of it she shared with no one except the strings and wind instruments that held a spirit of their own.

Symphony James was the maestro of her domain again. It was four a.m. on an unusually cold December morning, and Cadence was spending a few days with her grandparents. Symphony was already wrist deep in ingredients that her skilled hands would produce into a new pastry as delicate as dandelion fluff. She looked around at the kitchen she loved—the space that gave her life. This was what she knew—the smells, the sounds, the silky texture of the dough that she could read like a blind man reading braille. She knew this place, and Lord how she'd missed it.

In six short months, the life Symphony knew before she'd left Florida for Louisiana was gone. The empty spaces in her home were now filled with signs of motherhood. The spaces on her walls were filled with portraits of Cadence. But the largest space—the one in her heart, was now filled with the love for her daughter.

The happiness, heartache, headaches, and the sometimes hell she endured in her past found their designated places in her mind too. She recalled her memories with better clarity than before. She remembered all the days and nights she'd spent with Terry in her aunt's bakery, the walks, the talks, the silence filled only with the confidence of his love for her.

She remembered the way he'd looked at her when she laughed, the way he'd said her name when they greeted one another. She remembered how her eyelids closed when he stroked the back of his hand down her face and the subtle whiff of his cologne at unexpected moments. She remembered his kisses hello and the ones before they said good-bye.

Symphony also remembered, not so fondly, Terry's trips to meet with companies who were looking to train young bright men right out of college. She remembered her fear of losing him. She remembered the phone call that pushed him away. And she also remembered the pain that pushed her away from everyone else.

She recalled what a bitch she'd been and couldn't help but look at the door separating her kitchen from the front of the shop. A separation of happiness and heartache. It was what her customers and sales girls thought, anyway. Because clearly a woman must be suffering the death of love and rejection to be the bitch who lived in the kitchen.

Yes, she'd been a bitch. But it wasn't love that made her that way. It had taken her all this time to realize that despite how her parents treated her, love had been shared with her freely. Aunt Helen loved her more than like a cherished niece, but like a beloved daughter. Terry worshiped her and gave her more attention and affection than she'd known what to do with. All her life she'd wanted love so fiercely that fear of losing it kept her from accepting Terry's completely. But Kyle. She couldn't really describe how he loved her. She just knew that he did. He made her feel safe, comfortable, and well…whole.

Symphony sighed deeply, wiped her hands from the towel tucked in her apron strings, and went about the task of gathering ingredients for a new filling. She needed something perfect to go with the delicate pastry that she would turn into beautiful powder-dusted puffed ornaments.

That'd get their tongues to wagging.

By the time anyone arrived, the display case would look like Santa, himself, had come to decorate.

As for her own romance, she'd been too exhausted and overwhelmed to worry about filling that space. Terry Phoenix was back in Boston. She hadn't seen him since she'd left Baton Rouge. There was no doubt in Symphony's mind of Terry's feelings for her. Yet, he hadn't voiced them since the day Cadence went missing.

Her chest tightened just thinking about that day. But it was over. It was all over. They were rescued on the runway at a small airport in Houston, before the jet even took off. FBI officers were waiting on the jet owned by an air charter company. Never would she have thought Eric capable of kidnapping, but he was and almost succeeded if it hadn't been for Terry's family. Ethan and Landon's connections saved their lives. Law enforcement, local and federal, were convinced he couldn't have accomplished his plans alone. Someone must have funded his kidnapping plot, but they could not link him to anyone yet. Eric was killed trying to escape.

Why?

That was the question everyone asked. What had driven Eric to kidnapping? It was discovered that over the past ten years, three former girlfriends filed restraining orders against him, claiming he'd stalked them, and they were worried for their safety.

When federal officials searched his home, they found nothing. It was another reason they felt there was another party involved. No electronics were found, even though he had internet and Wi-Fi set up. The theory was that he must've been trying to blackmail someone, and they got to his place before the feds did.

What they did find were empty pill bottles—prescriptions for depression, mood stabilizers, and distorted thinking. Apparently, Eric was a total psychotic mess. There were also pictures of her all over his small home. The home he'd recently purchased in Jacksonville with a substantial down payment, though he'd been fired from a phone customer service job, six months before.

His walls were covered with information about her—what time she went to work, the location of her property inherited from her aunt, who worked at Symphony's and on what days, as well as a date scrawled in huge letters above his bed. After a while, Symphony realized it was the last day she'd met with him—the day she'd told him they were done. He'd wanted more than what she wanted to give anyone. And for that, he'd nearly destroyed her entire life.

How had she forgotten the pictures Cooper Read tried to blackmail her with? They were of Eric and her during the times she met him at a hotel. The police didn't know if Read had anything to do with the kidnapping or if he'd just been a convenient piece in Eric's game nearly a year ago.

Symphony pushed the awful episode from her mind. She did, however, realize that it was from the events of the kidnapping that she discovered how much Terry genuinely loved her. He'd gone away, but before he left, he said, "I know you need a minute right now with all you have going on. I don't want to be one more thing you have to worry about, so I'm taking myself out of the picture and giving you some space. When you're ready to let me love you like you know I can, I'll be wherever you need me to be."

He'd called several times, but he wasn't pressing her for an involvement. Apparently, Kyle was taking the same road as Terry. He hadn't pushed her into trying to be a family, but his eyes did nothing to conceal the depths of his feelings.

So far, he'd been great at helping with Cadence. He was over at least three times a week to visit with them both and would sometimes pick her up to spend time with Cadence at his own place in Daytona. At least once a month, Cadence spent the weekend with her grandparents.

Symphony knew that many single mothers would not grant a father so much access to their baby, but she wanted Cadence to know her family. Kyle's family were the only ones she had.

It wasn't long before Symphony was done with huge trays of strawberry-and-chocolate-filled round pastries. She'd also tried her hand at creating a savory breakfast tartlet with the leftover dough. Just before it was time for Ian to arrive, she'd placed what she could in the display out front and arranged plates of the savory items for people to sample. If they liked them, she would add them to the menu.

The outer back door opened, and then the one that led to the kitchen. If Ian was surprised to see her, he didn't show it. Normally he would have been there long ago, but Tuesday was his late arrival day. Ricco was supposed to be doing the morning prep, but Symphony phoned her the night before to tell her not to come in until later. She hadn't wanted to bother Ian. He'd been running the shop on his own since her aunt died.

Ian quickly washed up, donned his apron and hat, and checked on the pastries Symphony already had in the oven, and then he started boxing the large pre-orders and the to-go assortment boxes.

"Symphony, I'm glad you're here." She started at his sudden appearance at her side. She was wiping down the stainless-steel tables and didn't hear him approach.

"Damn it, Ian! You scared the crap out of me!"

He just stood there with his same indifferent appearance. He looked taller, paler, and leaner than usual, if that was even possible. After she composed herself, she realized he was waiting for a response. "Yes, Ian. What is it?" She placed the towel on the table and waited.

"I'm unable to go to the ABA conference this weekend." The American Baker's Association conference was one of those things that Symphony had gladly passed off to Ian when he'd expressed an interest. She hated conferences. "I'm so sorry, but it completely slipped my mind, and it's too late to get our money back. The flight is refundable, but we are one of the vendors providing deserts for several functions. If we don't show up, I'm afraid it would damage our reputation. Ricco, of course, is still able to attend."

She'd forgotten that Symphony's was a special vendor this year.

"When is it, exactly?"

"It begins Thursday afternoon and goes through Saturday. I've made all the arrangements to have what we need shipped there and have made sure we have a kitchen to use at the appropriate times."

166

"Shit, *this* Thursday?" That meant she'd have to make arrangements for Cadence.

"Yes, I'm terribly sorry, Symphony, but I can't change my plans."

"What's so important that you're missing the convention? I know how you love them." Ian thrived on being in the thick of other bakers and vendors, which made her curious about what would make him miss it.

"I have to fly to Hawaii Friday morning."

She knew that's where he was from. "Is everything ok?" He'd rarely gone home, usually just for the Christmas holidays. It was just the beginning of December; he'd never left this early in the month. She wondered if one of his parents were ill or worse. He'd never been one to share much about himself, but he wasn't a spontaneous "I'll just fly to Hawaii" kind of guy.

"I'm getting married."

If Ian had said he was going to find the end of the rainbow with Tupac, she wouldn't have been more surprised.

"Married?" Her mouth refused to shut.

"Yes." He stood there like he'd just told her he was going to get groceries. "I'll be back for my usual shift Monday morning." He normally did not work weekends, so technically, he was only taking off a day.

"Franny and Ishmel will be here Thursday, Friday, and Saturday. They have proven to be very reliable over the past several months."

Still, she could not speak. "I'm sorry I have not spoken with you about the conference before now. If needed, I will shorten my time in Hawaii and attend day one and two of the conference. I only need to be there by six p.m. Saturday for the ceremony."

She shook her head from side to side. "You mean to your wedding?" Unfortunately, she was not shocked about the absurdity of his comment. "Ian! You will do no such thing!" She wanted to shake him. "You will not just show up just in time for your ceremony and hop on a plane to return home the next day." That wasn't even time enough to consummate the marriage properly. Symphony couldn't believe her ears. She stepped past him. "Come with me to my office, please."

Symphony walked over to her desk, sat, and pulled out her company checkbook. Ian stood in the doorway. "Sit down, Ian," she said without looking up at him. He did as he was told.

"Symphony, I—" She held up a hand to silence him. It had taken him a very long time to call her by her first name. For the longest time, it had been "Ms. James," or just "ma'am," which she absolutely hated.

The only sound in the small office was her pen scratching across the paper, and then the perforated sound of the check being torn out.

"First, I cannot believe I didn't know you were getting married." She hadn't even known he was dating someone. "Is this someone you've known a while."

"Yes."

She waited for him to continue, but he said nothing else. She wondered then about something that hadn't occurred to her. "Do I have to worry about trying to replace you, Ian?"

"No, Symphony. I love working here. Alana will return with me."

"That's her name, Alana?"

"Yes." He stated, and suddenly a smile spread across his face that lit his eyes. "It means 'beauty' in Gaelic."

"It's a beautiful name."

"I promise everything is taken care of through Monday, just in case I am a little later than usual." He blushed. "But I will be back Monday morning, for sure."

"You will do no such thing. You will take this for all you've done for me and for this shop, and you will enjoy your new bride, and I don't want to see you for at least two weeks." Symphony handed him the check.

He took it hesitantly and looked at the amount. Eyes widening, he looked up at her. She held up a hand. "Ian, you deserve that and more. Congratulations!" She got up and walked around to him. He stood, and she gave him a big hug, which was uncharacteristic for both of them. She was surprised by the strength of the hug he returned. Her eyes were glassy. They both took a step back. She placed her hands on his shoulders. "Seriously, dude. I couldn't do this without you. I just want you to know that you are appreciated. When you return, we're going to talk about a permanent partnership."

He staggered and stared at her. "What?"

"You heard me. We'll talk about you owning a portion of Symphony's."

He looked so stunned that Symphony worried he would faint. Then suddenly Symphony was lifted off her feet and swung around. She squealed in surprise. So, Mr. Ian Palser was actually human after all.

Just then they both noticed a figure in the doorway. It was Marylyn, one of the girls who worked the counter. Symphony always referred to them as girls because they were so full of giggles and whispers all the time, but they were actually young women. She figured Marylyn and Stephanie were both in their early twenties, no kids or husbands. She wasn't sure if either had a boyfriend.

Ian and Symphony still had silly grins on their faces but were no longer touching. They looked at Marylyn, waiting for her to speak. But apparently, the woman was too overwhelmed to speak. She kept opening her mouth then closing it, then opening it again.

Symphony questioned her presence. "Yes, Marylyn?" Marylyn looked from Ian to Symphony. Symphony rolled her eyes and barked, "What!" The woman turned the color of her red hair.

"I—I just wanted to say that the pastries on the counter are very good." She finally found her voice to say. "The customers are going to love them."

Ian looked at Symphony with a question.

"I tried my hand at something new this morning. I put some out for the customers to sample, to see if we want to put them on the menu…A new type of Symphony's Originals."

171

He nodded and took a step forward, as if to leave. "Marylyn, did you know that Ian is getting married this weekend?" Symphony only asked to tease Ian, to get back at him for picking her up. The way Marylyn's breath hitched, and the way her eyes rounded before turning into slits directed at Ian, told Symphony that she did not know. She didn't seem to be pleased about it.

Symphony looked from Ian to Marylyn. To her surprise, again, Ian had a trace of guilt flitter across his features. Marylyn wore a full-on glare before saying, "No, I didn't." Her eyes never left Ian. "I hope you're very happy." Every word came out wrapped in barbed wire. Marylyn spun around and hit the door separating the kitchen and guest area so hard that it took a full fifteen seconds to stop swinging.

Symphony turned to Ian and raised a brow. She didn't even want to know what that was all about. Ian looked as if he was about to provide an explanation. She held up a hand. "Nope. Not my business. You take that $5,000 and go enjoy yourself. We have the shop until you get back." Symphony's head nodded toward the kitchen. Ricco was in there doing her usual morning duties. "I mean it, Ian. I don't want to see you in here for at least two weeks."

Symphony walked back to her chair at her desk and sank into it. She needed a moment in her office alone, to wrap her head around going to the conference and trying to figure out what to do with Cadence. Of course, Kyle or his parents wouldn't hesitate, but what if they already had weekend plans? Cadence was already spending the next two nights with them. But before she called Kyle or Pixie, she yelled out to Ian. "Where's the conference this year?" Maybe she would take a day or so and do some Christmas shopping for Cadence and her grandparents. Would it seem rude if she didn't get Kyle anything? Maybe she could get something for him from Cadence. She took a deep breath. She was getting ahead of herself and stressing for no reason.

She looked out toward the kitchen. She wondered if Ian hadn't heard her.

"Boston," he said, popping his head back into the office. "All the information is in that purple folder on your desk."

Boston.

Of course, it would be in Boston.

Chapter Twenty-One

The first day of the convention was exhausting. Why she'd let Ricco talk her into going out for drinks afterward, when all she wanted to do was crawl into the pillow-piled bed, she had no idea. Especially since they had to be up so early in the morning to set up for the breakfast exhibit.

Symphony heard a knock on her hotel room door. "Who is it?" She yelled out as she fastened the strap on her shoe.

"Ricco."

"Give me a sec."

Symphony fastened the shoe, grabbed her small bag, and gave herself one final check in the mirror. Just a light touch of makeup to hide the fatigue in her eyes, black jeans that showed off her new curves since the baby, and a red sparkly shirt that showed more cleavage than she was used to—that too, was new. She fluffed up her curly auburn locks that now hung past her shoulders and swung the door open.

She stared open-mouthed at Ricco. "Naricco Maki! You clean up well." Ricco wore a snug fitting, short black leather skirt with an off-the-shoulder white top with long sleeves that flared at the ends. Her long, sleek ebony hair hung to her lower back. "You look stunning!"

Ricco put her hand on her hip and gave Symphony a sassy stance before saying, "You don't look so bad, yourself, boss."

Ricco had always looked exceptionally tiny in her work clothes and hat, but the five-inch silver heels allowed the two women to nearly see eye to eye. It suddenly hit Symphony that she didn't know much about her employees outside of work. The only thing she knew about Ricco was that she'd grown up in Japan and had come to the States for college. Somehow, she'd ended up in Florida and had taken a job at the bakery, not long after Symphony opened her shop.

They took a seat at the bar in the hotel. From the delicious aromas mingling around them, Symphony hoped they could get dinner here also. The place was elegant. The bar area was huge, with muted lighting. The rest of the place was curvy and had comfortable seating. There were some areas that couldn't be seen from the entrance. A perfect place for a first date or if you needed a private spot to meet. The music was upbeat, but not too loud where a couple couldn't have a conversation. Nice place. Not really a compromise spot, after all.

Symphony was willing to go out anywhere Ricco wanted to go, as long as it was in the hotel. Ricco wasn't thrilled but had conceded since they had work in the morning, even though all the prep was done. She made sure to point that out.

It was also the first time Symphony had been out since before she was pregnant. Plus, she was getting a chance to hang out with another woman, which was something she rarely did.

Symphony pulled her phone out of her small bag and sat it on the smooth bar top. "Sorry, I need to make sure I can hear the phone in case Kyle calls me about Cadence."

"Kyle's your boyfriend?"

"He's Cadence's father."

Ricco looked down the bar. "Where's the bartender?" She turned back to give Symphony a pointed stare. "You didn't answer the question," she stated, before trying to get the bartender's attention.

It wasn't so much that Symphony thought Ricco's question was personal and none of her business, which she did, but it was a question that she'd been purposely avoiding answering herself. She honestly didn't know what Kyle was to her, other than

176

Cadence's father. Like Terry, Kyle had backed off on pushing for a relationship. They were too busy trying to figure out how to be parents.

"He's not my boyfriend."

"Do you have a boyfriend?"

"No." She felt confident in saying, then decided to turn the tables on Ricco. "Do you?"

"Nah."

That surprised Symphony. Ricco was gorgeous, seemed to be outgoing, and was smart as a whip. Which was why she'd planned on giving Ricco more duties at the shop and promoting her to manager. Symphony hadn't said anything to anyone, but she was seriously considering opening another store in Boston, as Alex had suggested. More like begged her. At any rate, she'd been doing her homework on the area.

"I've dated a few times, but nothing ever stuck."

"Why?"

"Most guys' idea of a good time is hanging out late, and with the hours I work, well…you know how that goes."

She didn't really, because her romantic history was less than ideal.

"Oh."

"Hey!" Symphony raised her brows. "Since you insisted on our evening be limited to this hotel bar, let's at least agree to do something we've never done before.

"What are you talking about?" she asked, with a confused chuckle.

"Let's make the night interesting by doing something we've never done."

"Like what?"

Ricco's forehead creased, and she made a real show of thinking about the question. "I don't know…like buying a guy a drink." She looked down the bar and back at Symphony. "Have you ever bought a guy a drink?"

"You mean a stranger?"

"Yeah."

"No." Symphony frowned.

"Well, that's just an example. It can be anything." Ricco was literally bouncing in her seat with her enthusiasm.

It was a natural instinct for Symphony to rebuff Ricco's attempt at fun, but just hanging out with Ricco was something she'd never really done before…and so far, she *was* having fun. The promise of a giddy girl's night out unfurled the knots that bound her impulses to be so serious all the time.

"Ok," she said, with an acquiescent smile.

They both giggled as the bartender approached. They ordered drinks, and Symphony was surprised at how easily conversation came between the two of them. She found out that Ricco spoke four languages, and of all things, could compute huge numbers in her head. She was some sort of math wizard—a gift Ricco considered a curse. Symphony recalled that whenever Ricco helped with the inventory, the task went much faster.

"Why aren't you an accountant?"

"Not computing numbers in my head is something I really have to work at. I mean, like hours and hours of Yoga and other types of meditation to not focus on numbers so much. It can literally drive a person crazy." She placed the tiny straws in her mouth and took a long pull on her drink. "I'm not saying I couldn't look over your books, for instance, and stay sane, I just don't want to do it for a living."

To Symphony, who was just ok at math but not great at it, couldn't fathom being so great at something that it could actually be a curse.

"I'm sure I asked you this in the interview, but why Symphony's?"

"I wanted to do what I love."

"Prep?"

"I love to bake. We have to start somewhere. I figure that after a while I'll get a chance to step up to the plate and do some serious baking. By that, I mean creating my own desserts. Or at the very least, making yours continue to taste perfect."

Symphony studied Ricco for a long moment. Her decision to open a new place couldn't be clearer if a billboard had been dropped in her lap. "Do you want your own place?"

"Nah." Ricco waved away the idea. Symphony was about to ask her something else when Ricco started bouncing in her seat to the thump-thump of the new song filling the area, her straw glued to the corner of her mouth as she siphoned the drink. "That's never been my goal…too much pressure, ya know?"

"Pressure?"

Ricco patted Symphony's forearm frantically. "Oh my gosh, Sym, look at those guys down there."

Sym?

She wasn't sure how she felt about being so casually referenced as "Sym," but she looked the way Ricco was blatantly gawking.

She saw two men sitting at a table with what looked like a contract between them. She could only see the face of one man. They were deep in conversation—most-likely conducting business.

Oh my!

Ricco had good cause to be struck dumbfounded. If a man could be called gorgeous, the man facing her could wear the description as a cape. Even from the distance of about forty feet away, Symphony could tell the man's eyes were a distinctive color. They were so piercing that it almost looked as if lasers were shooting from them. His hair was cut neatly—dark with streaks of silver. More silver than dark. The charcoal business suit was expensive and tailored just for him, the epitome of a successful businessman. She was certain, though, that even in rags the man would still be uncommonly handsome, no, absolutely gorgeous.

On cue, Symphony and Ricco turned to look at each other, wide-eyed, mouths agape, speechless.

"I wonder what the other one looks like," Ricco said in a hushed whisper. "Men like that usually travel in packs." Ricco's face lit with excitement. "Let's do it, Symphony!" Ricco's excitement made her feel giddy as well.

"Do what?"

"Send them drinks."

"What? No-oo…"

"C'mon, girl. You know you want to. And you promised you would do something you've never done."

"You said that was just an example."

"Well, the opportunity has presented itself."

Ricco signaled the bartender, and before Symphony could protest, she said, "We want to send those two guys over there another round." She pointed discreetly over Symphony's shoulder.

Symphony covered her face with her hands. "My God, Ricco, I'm going to stuff you in an oven!" After a few minutes, she spread her fingers, peeked through, and crooked her neck toward the pair. A waitress walked up to the men with the small tray that held a short glass of amber liquid, a bottle of dark beer, and a frosted glass. The men looked up at the waitress. The man that she could see tried not to look annoyed, but Symphony knew that look. Confusion clouded his features before the waitress pointed toward the bar where they sat. Symphony quickly turned a heated face toward Ricco.

Ricco leaned over and waggled her fingers. Not even as a girl had Symphony acted like what people would call a "silly girl." She'd been serious all the time and never really let herself do something daring, impractical, or fun. She didn't want to, but she had to admit, this was exhilarating.

Ricco patted the bar. "They're coming!"

"And then what?"

"O-M-G…they are both gorgeous." She gushed, ignoring Symphony's question. Ricco turned her stool toward the approaching men. Ricco's face and smile was as composed as Symphony's nerves were frazzled.

Symphony turned and looked up into the face of Captain Gorgeous, and just as he said, "Hello," to the both of them, another voice came from behind her—a voice she knew.

Chapter Twenty-Two

"Symphony?"

Symphony turned, and her gaze collided with the one person she'd hope to avoid while she was in town. She was still at a loss with where to place him in her life.

"Terry?" She was just as surprised to see him as he was to see her.

Something that had the markings of disappointment and hurt hooded his expression. It was brief, but she saw it.

"You seemed surprised." His left eye squinted slightly—something he did when he was perplexed and angry.

Why the hell would he be angry? The drinks?

His eyes brushed Ricco, who was sitting expectantly and looking from Symphony to Terry. "You didn't know it was me." The words were more of an accusation than a statement.

Ah…She got it now. He figured she was trying to pick up a guy in a bar. Shit! This was not turning out to be the whimsical night she envisioned. Symphony cocked a brow at him, lifted her chin, not giving a damn what he thought. She was not his. What they had was over. She was free to explore her options. She turned to the other guy and stuck out her hand. "Hi, I'm Symphony James, and this is my colleague, Naricco Maki."

The man smiled pleasantly at Symphony as he took her hand in his. His eyes! She'd never seen eyes like his before. They were damn near metallic silver— lightning trimmed in fine dark halos. The intensity of them held her. She swore he could see her soul and all the dark places that were hidden there.

"Hello, Ms. James." His voice was so soothing, she could feel herself slipping into the comfort of it from just those few words. Ricco cleared her throat, and Symphony realized she was looking up at the man, wide-eyed and dumbfounded. A shiver ran through her when he released her hand. She didn't like it. If she'd been watching this scene play out in a movie, she would peg the man for something not of this world.

He turned to Ricco. She seemed to have the same reaction that Symphony had.

"Ms. Maki," he said to Ricco, still holding her hand.

Symphony could actually feel the charge radiating between the two.

"Thank you for the drink."

"You're welcome, but we didn't mean to interrupt…and call me Ricco, please."

"Nice to meet you both." His eyes pinned them. "I'm Kenny Cavanaugh." To Ricco, he said, "This is Terry Phoenix. We conduct a little business from time to time."

Ricco tore her eyes away from the man to look between Symphony and Terry. "Do the two of you know each other."

Whatever Terry was about to say was cut off by Symphony's reply, "We met in college, and I'm friends with the wife of Terry's cousin." Symphony looked up at Terry. "How is Alex and Joshua?"

"They're both fine. They should be in town in a day or two." He turned to Ricco. "I'm sorry, I didn't mean to appear rude. Like this one just said," he pointed a thumb toward Kenny, "I'm Terry."

Terry and Kenny both held the drink that was sent over to them.

"Would you ladies like to join us?" It was Kenny who spoke.

"Oh no, we don't want to disturb you." Symphony declined at the same time Ricco replied, "Sure, we'd love to."

Kenny looked at them both and smiled. Terry looked as if he didn't know what the hell to do.

Symphony didn't know how this would play out, but what the hell, she was in ankle deep now.

"Here or our table? Kenny asked. "We were just about to stop to order dinner."

"In that case, we'll go to your table," Ricco replied, taking the hand Kenny offered as he helped her off the stool. Symphony wanted to roll her eyes, but she plastered on a smile as she let Terry help her from the stool as well. Even though she was perfectly capable of getting down on her own.

What the hell was she doing? She would have another drink and excuse herself with the excuse that she had to get up early.

A waitress appeared the instant they were seated at the table. Kenny asked for menus. The moment Symphony's eyes scanned the menu, her stomach reminded her that it had been several hours since it was last visited by any type of worthwhile sustenance. She thought about going up to her room and ordering room service. She could feel Terry's eyes on her. She looked at him fully. To hell with it. She was going to enjoy her night, Terry Phoenix be damned.

And she did.

They all did.

Symphony could tell that Ricco was becoming quite taken with Mr. Kenny "Lightning Eyes" Cavanaugh.

The conversation flowed smoothly between them. Terry wasn't sitting any closer to her than Kenny, but she found herself pressing his upper arm or patting his hand when she spoke about places near her home. When had she become so touchy-feely?

Do you remember the time when we… or *Terry and I had a professor that…*

It was an unconscious occurrence that she didn't know she was doing until after she'd done it. She realized that she'd missed him. Missed the easy banter they once shared.

Symphony listened to Terry tell Ricco about a neighborhood their company was in the process of revitalizing. Ricco was fascinated. They both were. She'd never really known what Terry did. Could be because she'd been trying so hard to push him away that she hadn't realized he'd grown into a man and was no longer the college boyfriend she'd known so long ago.

"What are you doing to prevent gentrification in the neighborhood?" Ricco asked him.

Symphony knew that many times, neighborhoods were given a facelift by adding new shops and businesses, along with more upscale housing, essentially pushing out the original population because they could no longer afford to live in the area.

"If anything, we're offering more affordable housing in better conditions. The previous landlords were bleeding the tenants dry and offering nothing in return."

"What do you mean?"

"They provided a space for them to live and run their businesses, but landlords did nothing to keep the structures viable. People who'd lived in the neighborhood all their lives were forced to move out of the area completely, usually with family, or they were simply forced to the streets because they couldn't afford rent and upkeep."

"It's never simple to be forced to the streets." Ricco made the statement with such vehemence that all eyes turned to her. A heaviness settled over the table, and the absence in Ricco's eyes, told them her thoughts had traveled elsewhere.

Terry flicked a glance at Symphony, and then back to Ricco. Symphony again, wished she'd taken more moments to get to know the people who worked for her. There was a depth to Ricco that she never knew existed.

"No, Naricco, it is not simple at all to find yourself with no place to go." It was Kenny who finally spoke, his voice filled with quiet compassion.

Ricco looked at Kenny for a very long time—her eyes searching his. She gave an imperceptible nod before excusing herself to go to the restroom. The two men stood when she did.

"I'd better go check on her," Symphony said.

Not long after they returned, Symphony announced that she and Ricco needed to get some sleep, because they had a very early morning. Ricco didn't want to talk about it, but the conversation with Terry had upset her somehow.

Symphony turned to them. "It was good seeing you again, Terry." And she meant it. "And it was nice meeting you, Kenny."

"Maybe before the two of you leave the city, we can meet again," Kenny said, his eyes never leaving Ricco.

"Well, we'd better get going," Symphony said, never committing to meeting again.

It wasn't that she didn't want to. It was that she did want to, and she didn't know what to do with that feeling. She was about to walk away when Terry pulled her into a soft embrace, placed a chaste kiss near her ear, and whispered, "You know you want to."

She didn't know if it was her hormones still trying to normalize or the fact that she hadn't had sex in over a year, but those words and the warmth of his breath at her ear sent a volt to the juncture of her thighs—reminding her that she was way overdue for some sexual maintenance.

On shaky legs, it was in her best interest to just walk away.

The conference was a great success. The business contacts were promising and supported her idea of opening a shop in Boston. On a whim, Symphony and Ricco made several savory items that were a huge winner. They flew off the platters. She knew they were items that she'd have to keep on her menu.

Terry's revitalization project would not leave her mind. She wanted to talk to him about an idea she had.

Chapter Twenty-Three

Terry wanted to see Symphony before she left, but he'd decided six months ago that he would put the ball in her court. If she wanted to see him, she'd have to initiate it.

The other night when he realized one of the ladies who'd sent over the drinks was Symphony, jealousy and anger sliced through him. He was equally relieved when he found out the circumstances behind the act.

Terry hadn't liked the feeling and was even more angry with himself for pining over a woman who hadn't given him the time of day since the day she'd called and told him it was over.

He was such a fool for wanting her, and he knew it. He'd waited over seven years for her and felt that it was about time she knew he wouldn't wait forever. He wanted the works—career, wife, kids, and a dog sitting at his feet in the suburbs. If Symphony James didn't want the same with him, it was time for him to move on. The nagging voice in his head kept telling him that she already had a kid.

With. Another. Man.

What a fool love had made him. He thought again.

Terry's phone buzzed. "Mr. Phoenix?"

"Yes, Jasmine."

"Mr. Powers says he's not going to be able to make lunch today. Something came up." He and Ethan always had lunch on Mondays.

"Ok, Jasmine. Thanks." He stood, not sure what he wanted to do.

Walking to the window he wondered what had come up. Just a few hours ago, Ethan had been eager to go to their favorite lunch spot. Terry reached for his phone to call Symphony to see if she was free for lunch and remembered the stance he'd taken.

Shit.

"You're such an idiot, Phoenix," he said aloud, squeezing the cell phone in his hand. He went back to his desk to buzz his secretary.

"Yes, Mr. Phoenix."

"Will you have something delivered to the office from the deli."

"Sure, sir. What would you like?"

"Surprise me."

"Sir?"

He rolled his eyes. Jasmine was not the "surprise me" kind of girl. He needed a new office assistant, but he never had the strength to break in someone new, so he just put up with Jasmine. She wasn't horrible, but she wasn't a person who was quick on her feet. "Just get me ham and provolone on a tomato basil bread."

"Yes, sir." She hesitated. "Would you like mayo or mustard on it?" Never had he ordered a sandwich with mustard. He pinched the bridge of his nose. "Mayo…lettuce, tomato, a pickle on the side, and the house chips."

"I'll order it right away." She hung up.

Terry was quite certain she would not order the Diet Coke that he had with the sandwich every time he ordered it, because he didn't specifically say he wanted it. Terry called her back after a few minutes passed. "Will you please get me a Diet Coke."

"Sure, I'll call them right back."

He rolled his eyes, opened a file on his desk, and did his best not to think about Jasmine or Symphony James.

Work consumed him for the next couple of hours, and he was glad.

His phone buzzed again.

"Mr. Phoenix, Mr. Phoenix is here."

He closed his eyes in frustration. "Jasmine, there are several 'Mr. Phoenixes' that works for this company. It is called Phoenix Industries. You will need to be more specific, and there really is no need to announce any of them unless I'm in a meeting."

"Yes, sir. It's Landon Phoenix."

"Send him in," he gritted out.

Landon walked in, a mischievous glint in his eyes. He'd done that on purpose. He knew how much his office assistant irritated him. "You absolutely did that on purpose."

"Yes… yes I did."

"Clearly you don't have enough work to do. What do you want anyway?"

"I just stopped in to be nosey."

"You'll have to be more specific."

"You know what I'm talking about. I just saw her leave the floor."

"Who?"

"Symphony."

"What're you talking about? Symphony was here?"

"Yes, I figured she'd been in to see you."

"Well she wasn't." He picked up the file that he'd just finished reading. "So, if you're done being nosey, I have work to do."

"How long are you going to let this woman consume you?"

"You don't know what the hell you're talking about." Terry pushed away from the desk and stood. Landon stood too.

"I like Symphony and all, but damn Cuz, she had a kid with another dude. Your entire family helped her get the baby back when she was kidnapped, and still you're sitting here obsessing over her. She should be throwing herself in your arms.

"I just saw her getting on the elevator on this floor, and yet she didn't drop in to say hi to you." Landon stuck his hand in his pocket. "That speaks volumes to me, man."

"I appreciate you stopping by to check on me."

Landon threw up both hands. "Ok, dude. I'm out. But think about what I said."

Terry watched Landon stroll out of the office and fell back into his chair. What the hell was Symphony doing here, and why *hadn't* she stopped by his office?

His phone buzzed, again. "Yes!" The word came out harsher than he'd intended. He took a deep breath and adjusted his tone. "Yes, Jasmine?" he said, a bit softer.

"Mr. Powers is here to see you."

He sighed again. "Send him in, Jasmine. And you don't have to announce Ethan either."

"Yes, sir." She replied, but Terry knew she would do it again.

Ethan walked in and paused.

"What?" Terry asked.

"You cleaned off your desk?" It was no secret that Terry was the only one who could find anything in his office. Not even his secretary could sort through the chaos. His desk usually sat smothered under stacks of files and who knew what else. "You did that to impress Symphony?"

What the hell! Had everyone seen her except him? "Landon was just in here with his words of advice to me about Symphony. What do you have to add?"

Ethan was taken aback by Terry's tone.

"I don't know what you and Landon talked about, but I was just coming in to say that I thought her idea was a great one. It will be perfect for the neighborhood."

"Wait…What're you talking about?"

"She didn't tell you?" Landon took one of the seats in front of Terry.

"I saw Symphony by chance when I was meeting with Kenny the other night. We chatted, but I have no idea what you're talking about. And I had no idea she'd been here today until Landon told me."

"She said you'd told her about the revitalization project."

The revitalization project? His forehead creased, his expression perplexed. He and Symphony hadn't talked about business at all. Then he remembered talking to Ricco about rebuilding the neighborhood without allowing gentrification to set in. "I mentioned it in passing, but there was no real discussion. Why would Symphony come talk to you about it?"

"She wants Enrich Corp. to include her bakery in the neighborhood."

Now this bit of news was surprising. Enrich Corp. was a division of Phoenix Industries that was started by Ethan and Landon. Its main function was to find ways to help the environment and to increase the vitality of dying neighborhoods, all without displacing the people who'd been living in those areas all their lives.

Symphony wants to open a bakery in Boston? What did that mean?

"Why?"

"You'd have to ask her that. She does, however, have some great ideas to help the neighborhood."

Terry didn't want to ask Symphony anything. How dare she come to their company and not come to see him. And why did he have to find out about her wanting to open a new bakery from one of his cousins?

Because she's not yours. A voice kept screaming at him. *She is not obligated to tell you anything. When will you get that through your thick skull?*

"Hey, man, you ok? Ethan asked.

Before Terry could answer, Sophia breezed through the office door with her arm hooked through Symphony's.

"Looked who I found in the lobby!" she announced, before walking over to Ethan, still in his chair, planting a loud kiss on his mouth.

Terry rolled his eyes. He didn't think the two of them would ever get out of the newlywed stage. His phone buzzed on his desk.

"Mr. Phoenix, Mrs. Phoenix is here to see you. I know she's already in there, but you said to announce your visitors."

He didn't waste any effort to tell her that it was pointless to announce a person that was already in the office. "Thanks, Jasmine." He didn't know how long he could put up with her empty head.

"Symphony," Terry stated as blandly as he could without sounding cold. He stood but didn't move from behind his desk.

"Hello, Terry."

Ethan stood and looked at his watch. "Is it time to get Bridgett, already?" he asked Sophia. Bridgett was their nine-year-old adopted daughter.

Symphony turned to Sophia. "Are you leaving, Sophia? I thought we'd get a chance to do some shopping."

"I would have loved that, but Bridgett has a Christmas program at school today. And we promised to take her for hot chocolate afterward." Sophia hugged Symphony. "How long are you in town?"

Terry was curious to know this answer as well.

"I'm heading out tomorrow."

"Ah, chica! I'm sorry. You'll have to come around more often."

"I may just be doing that. I've decided to open a bakery here in Boston." She was answering Sophia but looking at Terry.

Sophia clapped her hands. "How exciting! That'll be wonderful, won't it Terry? I can feel myself gaining ten pounds just thinking about all the stuff I want to eat. I'll have to teach extra dance classes."

Terry added. "Yes, things must be going well for you, Symphony, to want to expand so far away from home."

For just a moment, the two were caught in their own thoughts and simply stared at each other. Neither noticed Ethan and Sophia leave the office.

"I'd heard you were in the building today," Terry said absently as he sat in his chair.

"Yes, I came by after speaking with Ethan, but your secretary said you were busy."

"She did? I didn't have any appointments today."

Symphony shrugged. "Well, that's what she said."

Terry took a huge breath and looked up to the ceiling as if searching for some sort of divine guidance in dealing with his office assistant. He was both irritated as hell and elated that Symphony had, in fact, planned to visit with him.

He reached for the phone. He gestured for Symphony to sit and pushed in an extension. The call was on speaker.

"Jasmine, why did you tell Ms. James that I was busy when she stopped by earlier?"

"I have on my calendar that you had a lunch meeting with Mr. Powers."

"Didn't you call me earlier to tell me that Mr. Powers canceled? And didn't I order in lunch today?"

"Well, yes, sir. I didn't think you wanted to be disturbed." Terry looked up at Symphony and saw her trying to keep herself from laughing. He smiled too. "Sir?"

"Thank you, Jasmine. That's all."

Terry's next call was to HR. "Tammy?"

"Yes, Mr. Phoenix?" Tammy had been with the company for years.

"Tammy, will you please find me another office assistant?"

There was a pause before Tammy responded. "Jasmine not working out for you?"

"No, ma'am. She's not."

"Are you firing her?"

"No, she's just not cut out to be an office assistant. Can you stick her in the mail room?"

"We've tried that, Mr. Phoenix, and it…well…it just didn't work out."

Terry shook his head, not surprised. "Find some place to put her and get me someone who can think on their feet." Tammy didn't say anything. "Please," he begged.

He heard her chuckle before she responded, "I'll get right on it. I think I have the perfect candidate for you."

When he hung up the phone, both he and Symphony burst into laughter.

Symphony wiped a tear from her eye. "I didn't mean to get the poor woman in trouble."

"You didn't. I've known for a while that she needed to be replaced, but I kept giving her chances. There's no telling how many important calls or meetings I've missed." He stood from his chair and sat on the corner of his desk. "If there's something really important that I'm working on, I get Leslie, the office manager for the floor, to handle things."

"I see."

He watched her look around his office and was actually glad he'd taken the time that morning to clear the chaos from his desk. He definitely couldn't have asked his secretary to do it.

"So, this is where you work."

"Yes." He spread his arms. "This is where the magic happens."

"Boston seems nice. From what I've seen so far."

"It is. Especially if you like history. I wish you had more time for me to give you a proper tour." He'd like to give her a tour of his townhouse too. There were a few places in it that he'd really like for her to get more acquainted with.

Terry felt the soft pull in his chest that he always felt when he looked at her. She was like a ghost. He never knew how long their moments together would last, or when he'd get to see her again.

"Are you free to show me the neighborhood you were talking about the other night, and maybe come with me to do some Christmas shopping for Cadence?"

Terry was so shocked that she'd asked him to join her that he was speechless for a moment.

"If you're busy or don't want to, I'm sure I could manage to get around by myself."

"No…no. I'm just surprised you asked. That's all." She nodded. "I'd love to show you around and do some shopping." The shopping, he could have done without, but it was an opportunity to spend some time with her, so he would take it. "Where's Ricco?"

"She was supposed to fly out this morning, but I'm not so sure if she did."

Terry raised his brows.

Symphony shrugged before Terry escorted her out of the office. When he passed Jasmine at her desk, he told her he would be out the rest of the day. She looked surprised and confused all at once. He hoped to God she would be gone by the time he arrived at work in the morning.

Chapter Twenty-Four

Symphony found out quickly that December in Boston was very different from December in Florida. Most days at home, she didn't even need a jacket until mid-January or February. The coat she wore should've been warm enough, but she still felt cold.

Symphony pulled the hat over her ears, her hair falling in loose curls around her face. The moment they stepped out into the brilliant sunshine of the cold and windy day, she wrapped her arms around herself and shivered. Terry pulled on his gloves, and like he had every right to do so, draped an arm around her, and pulled her into his side.

She told herself that it was only the frigid weather that kept her from pulling away. She snuggled up, willingly tucked in his strong arm. Years had passed, but the place was familiar.

"There's a place called Downtown Crossing. It's just a few blocks from here. Everyone shops there. I'm sure you'll find whatever you're looking for." They stopped at a crossing. "There are some great eating places there as well, if we get hungry later."

"Ok," she said, but she felt like he wasn't too sure about the place.

"It may be crowded."

"Most places are, this time of year." She was shivering a little and was very aware of his hand rubbing up and down her arm—much too aware. "Do you have someplace else in mind?"

"It's not as polished as Downtown Crossing, at least not yet, but there are a couple places in the old art district where we're renovating. It will be close to where your shop could possibly be."

"Yes, let's go there."

The neighborhood was not too far from the Phoenix offices, but it would have been a pretty good walk in the cold, so Symphony was glad when Terry said he would get his car. She knew immediately it was Terry when the new blue-gray Genesis drove up in front of the office building. The car suited him—very stylish yet understated.

"I love your car," she said, looking around the interior after she'd fastened her seatbelt. The seats felt like butter.

"Thanks."

"The new-car smell always makes me want to go to the lot, but my bank account keeps me grounded." He smiled as he maneuvered through traffic with ease. "How long have you had it?"

"I got it a few months ago. It was my gift to myself after closing a deal I'd worked hard securing."

"Must've been a big deal." She imagined he did pretty well for himself if this luxury car was a treat. A treat to her was a new outfit or some specialty ingredients she could use at home.

Symphony was pretty impressed with what she'd seen so far on the drive. Boston was nowhere near as overwhelming as New York, a place she'd only visited for business.

"It was a pretty big deal. The biggest of my career, so far. I was able to get this car and put a pretty hefty down payment on a house right outside of town."

She raised a brow. "Wow, Terry, that's great!" She was genuinely happy that things were going well for him. "Buying a house is a pretty big deal."

"Yeah, I figured it's time for me to start settling down."

What did he mean by that? Was he seeing someone? Was he ready to start a family? A twinge of anxiety caused her pulse to quicken. She looked at him and then out of the window again, wondering why she cared.

"I'm knocking on thirty's door, and I don't want to be an old man raising kids."

Damn. There it was. She was too afraid to look his way—too afraid to find out he was moving on.

Without her. Again.

Symphony thought about Cadence, and immediately a smile came to her face. She couldn't imagine a life without her.

"I think you'll make a great dad." She meant it.

"Yeah?"

She looked at him and nodded her head. She didn't trust herself to speak right then.

"Here we are." Symphony noticed that they were stopped along the street in front of a restaurant. "I parked here because maybe we can eat here later. But the place I was talking about before is a couple blocks down. We won't be able to get this parking spot in an hour or two. Ready?"

"Sure."

They both got out. Terry indicated which way they should walk. Symphony wasn't sure about this weather. She just wasn't used to sustaining winter temperatures. Latching on to Terry's arm, she convinced herself that it was the cold that made her want to hold on to him and absorb his warmth. It also didn't hurt that he smelled so damn good. The subtle cologne made her want to snuggle up with him on a sofa.

Her thoughts were taking her to places that she wasn't sure if she wanted to go with him. Her body begged to differ, but she tried like hell to ignore it.

"The name of your shop will fit perfectly in this artsy area."

"Think so?" They stopped so she could look in the window of an art gallery. It was one of many, she noticed. This one seemed to specialize in sculptures.

"Yes, it's perfect." He looked thoughtfully into her eyes. She held his. They were dark, daring, and the deep brown she remembered from so long ago. Her eyes fell to his lips, set in a slight smile, and she wasn't sure if it was the weather, the romantic feel of all the Christmas decorations and music filling the air from somewhere nearby, or if she'd temporarily lost her mind, but whatever the hell it was had her arms snaking around his shoulders. The next instant, her mouth was on his.

Damn the fact that they were on a semi-busy sidewalk in the middle of the day. Her tongue joined his in a dance that was so familiar, her entire body sighed with delight. It was Terry who pulled away first. Breathing hard, he rested his forehead on hers. He smiled, and she returned it with one of her own.

"What was that?" he asked, breath still coming out in short bursts.

"Well, in the south, we call it a kiss. What would you call it?"

"An awakening."

Now that, she had to agree with. Her entire being was awake and wanting way more than it could have in the middle of a sidewalk.

Symphony spotted a woman eyeing them with a knowing smile and raised eyebrow, figuring it was time for them to stop giving people a show. She pulled her forehead away, but Terry twirled a strand of her hair before pulling her back to him for the sweetest kiss she'd had in a very long time. The press of their lips was soft and promising. He pulled away, offered his elbow to her, and she latched on, the cold no longer an issue.

Symphony's body buzzed with heat. Her steps to the shop were accompanied by a pulsing in a place that seemed long forgotten. She tried like hell to get her body in check while Terry told her about the neighborhood. Unfortunately, she couldn't focus on anything he said. Though she didn't want them to, thoughts of Kyle creeped into her consciousness. It was difficult not to compare the two.

Terry's kiss was familiar and safe. But, Kyle's—

"Here it is," Terry announced, as they came to a stop. She looked up at the battered old sign that read "Arlene's Place."

"Will they have stuff for Cadence in here?"

"Yes. Arlene has everything—unique and not so unique things."

Symphony looked at the storefront with skepticism.

"Trust me. You'll love it."

She looked up at him. "I trust you."

Terry paused for a few moments before shaking himself briefly. She wondered what that was about but didn't ask him. As he reached for the door, he said, "As part of the neighborhood beautification project, all the store owners qualify for either grants or very low interest loans to spruce up the interior and exterior of their businesses."

Symphony thought that was pretty interesting. She stepped into the store and a small plump brown-skinned woman greeted them both. "Welcome to Arlene's Place."

Symphony smiled, too overwhelmed by the array of eclectic items all over the store.

"This is Symphony, Ms. Arlene. She's thinking about opening a bakery on the block."

"You aren't Symphony from *THE* Symphony's in St. Augustine?"

She was taken aback by the woman's recognition of her bakery. "Yes, ma'am, I am."

Arlene gave Symphony a tight hug of excitement. "Oh, my word! My sister Vivi and I make it a point to go there when we visit St. Augustine." She looked up at Terry. "And you say she's bringing her bakery to our neighborhood?"

"Yep."

"Lord, Henry will be so happy to know there will be no chance of me losing weight while your bakery is around."

"Henry?" Symphony asked.

"My husband. He just loves squeezing all my fluffy places." She waved a hand in exasperation. "I'm like his own little playground."

It took everything Symphony had to stifle a laugh. "Well, isn't that what you're supposed to be to each other?"

"I can't lie, honey. I can't keep my hands off him either. That's why he bought me this store…trying to keep me off him." Symphony did laugh then. She hoped her shop would be close enough so that she would see Arlene often. And then she wondered why the thought occurred to her when she hadn't planned on being in Boston for the everyday running of the store.

"Anything I can help you two find?" Arlene asked looking between Terry and Symphony. "Coming to buy something for the new house?" she asked, smiling up at the both of them.

Symphony spoke up, first. "I'm looking for something for my little girl for Christmas. She'll be seven months when Christmas comes."

Arlene didn't skip a beat. She tugged them both along to show them all the baby stuff. Symphony turned to Terry with a you-brought-me-here look on her face. Terry shrugged and allowed himself to be led.

Chapter Twenty-Five

"Terry, it's gorgeous!" Symphony exclaimed, looking around the beautifully decorated living room of Terry's new home.

"Let me show you the kitchen," he said, tugging her to follow him.

Her breath caught. It was her dream kitchen. She walked over to the massive stove with double ovens and wanted to hug it. The hanging pot rack was stocked with top-of-the-line cookware. The island was massive, with lots of electrical outlets for appliances. The kitchen was everything she would want in a kitchen. Hers was nice, of course. She paid extra for the builders to upgrade her appliances, but it was by no means custom.

"It's beautiful, Terry. I mean just absolutely perfect." Her hand rubbed along the stove's buttons and knobs. Terry leaned casually against a counter. "It's gas." Her words still laced with a tinge of awe.

"Yes. I remember you telling me not to ever buy a house if it didn't have a gas stove."

She smiled at the memory and turned to face him. He was much closer than she thought. He was an arm's length away. She knew, because in that moment, he reached for her and pulled her to him.

Symphony hesitated at first, before allowing him to pull her close. He placed his forehead on hers like on the sidewalk. "I've missed you, Symphony James."

She really didn't know what to say to that. Did she miss him too? Or had she just missed being touched by a man? "Do you think it means something that I couldn't remember my life after you when I lost my memory?" She needed to know.

"Do you think it means something?"

"I'm not sure," she whispered. All she had was honesty. She lowered her head, and his chin rested on it.

"I've always loved the scent of your shampoo." She smiled.

"Today, on the sidewalk," she began, trying not to let his cologne intoxicate her. "That kiss. What was that?"

"That was us, Symphony," he said simply.

Symphony's phone rang from her purse in the other room. From the ringtone, she knew it was Pixie. "I need to get that."

Symphony ran to the sofa where she'd laid her purse. "Hello? Pixie?"

"Hi, honey. I hope I'm not interrupting anything."

"No, you're not. Is anything wrong?"

"There's nothing to be alarmed about. I just wanted to let you know Cadence has a slight fever. She's been teething. I just wanted to make sure I can give her some Tylenol."

"How high is it?" Symphony looked up when Terry walked in the room.

"Anything wrong?" he whispered.

Symphony shook her head, but he didn't seem to believe her because he kept walking toward her.

"Oh, it's just 100.2. I only called to make sure she isn't allergic to anything before I give her something for the pain and fever."

"No, she's not. Are you sure she's ok?"

"Yes, sweetie."

"Is that her?" Symphony could hear Cadence laughing in the background.

"Yes. Kyle is singing some silly little song to her—to distract her."

"Oh." What song? Symphony suddenly felt like she was missing so much being away from her daughter. Kyle was making her laugh, and frankly she was jealous that he had a silly little song to make her laugh. She knew she was being ridiculous, but she suddenly wished she was home.

"Ok, dear. Go on. We'll see you tomorrow."

"Ok. But the Tylenol is fine. You sure she's ok?"

"She's just going through what all babies go through at this age." She could hear the smile in Pixie's voice. She really loved Kyle's mom. Both his parents were great grandparents to her daughter. Cadence would grow up loved by so many.

"Ok. Well, kiss her for me."

"Ok, dear."

Pixie hung up, and Symphony held on to the phone, feeling left out.

Apparently, Terry realized the moment in the kitchen was gone. "Want to see the rest of the house?"

Suddenly, she felt left out of Terry's life too. He'd bought this big beautiful townhouse to one day fill with a wife and kids. She was just ready to go back to the hotel, so she could get ready to go home in the morning.

"Nah, I'd better get back to the hotel and make sure I'm ready. I have an early flight."

"Ok." He didn't sound disappointed, which made Symphony take another look at him.

"You sure you don't mind shipping my purchases to me?"

"Not at all. I'll send them out first thing in the morning."

The drive to the hotel was quiet. She'd planned on getting out at the front lobby doors, but there were still quite a few packages that she'd planned on taking with her, and Terry insisted on helping her up to her room.

Terry placed the packages just inside the door. "Nice room."

"Yes, it is," she replied, looking around as if it was her first time looking at it. When she'd first arrived, it felt quite spacious, but with Terry Phoenix standing in it, the room felt much smaller. She pulled off her coat and hat and placed them on a chair in the sitting area.

"You're flying back alone?"

"Yes, I stayed an extra day for business." She walked to the closet and pulled out her suitcase to see how she would stuff some of the new purchases in it, or if she would have to leave them with Terry.

"Why didn't you talk to me about your plans to open a new bakery?"

She looked up at him. There was something different in his tone. Symphony hadn't thought about how Terry would feel to hear about her plans from his cousin.

"I didn't want to mix business with my personal life."

He looked at her for a very long time. "I see," he stated flatly.

The intensity of his gaze made her heart beat faster. She had no idea why, but at that very moment, she wanted him to see her. To really see her. Not the woman he may have thought she was at one time, but the woman she was now. Flawed, sometimes insecure, vulnerable, regretful, strong, and determined. She wanted all the things he wanted. Love, a family, stability, a life free to grow old with someone. She just didn't know if she needed to go back to her past to secure that kind of future for herself.

"What do you see?" she gathered the nerve to ask.

"I see you," he said with assurance. He took a step forward.

Symphony took a step back. "What do you see?" Her voice was urgent and pleading.

"I see the woman I want."

At that very moment, she wanted to know what that felt like. To be wanted so completely that no one else could fill that space.

She stepped toward him, and he wasted no time gathering her into him.

"Thanks again for today, Terry." He pulled her closer and groaned.

There it was again. Whatever that thing was that captured them both on the sidewalk earlier. "I enjoyed shopping with you, Symphony." He breathed next to her ear. And he truly didn't seem to mind spending so much time at Arlene's and the other shops they'd visited before dinner. She'd helped him pick out things for his parents and other family members.

"Thank you for shopping with me." Her words brushed the curve of his neck, and she couldn't help herself when she placed a soft kiss there. His groan of pleasure fueled her to kiss him again.

"Symphony…" Her name a litany from his lips.

Terry shoved his hands in her hair and pulled her lips up to his. She could taste his desire for her—frantic and desperate. And she desperately wanted to be wanted.

Terry's hands slid along her side and gripped the bottom of her shirt. "Symphony." Her name spoken with such desperation startled her. "My dream girl." He murmured through his kisses.

Symphony remembered he'd once told her that he'd seen her in a dream. That it was fate that they be together.

His palms slid up the inside of her shirt, and the moment the heat of hands touched her bare flesh, she knew.

She knew without an equivocal doubt.

There was only one choice to make.

Chapter Twenty-Six

"How many times are you going to pick up that phone?" Warren asked.

Kyle looked at his dad, chagrined. He'd been checking to see if he'd missed a message from Symphony. She'd stayed an extra night in Boston. Kyle knew that the conference ended Sunday afternoon. He was surprised she didn't leave that evening, but she'd called saying she'd decided to stay an extra night to check on a business opportunity.

What business opportunity did she have in Boston? He wasn't too proud to admit that he was jealous. Not just jealous, but burning up with it, to know that Symphony was in the same city as a man who had admitted wanting her.

"Just checking to see if Symphony texted or called," he finally said to his dad.

"Doesn't that thing make a noise when either of those things happen?"

"Yes."

"What's eating you up, son?"

"Terry Phoenix lives in Boston."

223

Warren nodded, knowingly. "So, that's what's got you all twisted inside."

"The man told me that he's still in love with her and plans on having her back."

"And what did you say to that?"

"Pretty much, let the best man win."

"This isn't a game, son."

"I know that."

"Then why are you treating Symphony like she's some sort of chess piece you have to win?"

"I'm not."

"You should want her to be happy."

"I know, Dad, but Symphony and I have a chance to be a family."

"Would you love Cadence any less if you couldn't have Symphony too?"

"No."

"Would you love her more if you were living in the same house?"

"I love her more than I ever thought it possible to love a human being." Kyle watched his dad get up and walk to the kitchen.

"Come take a ride with your old man."

Warren yelled up to his mom to tell her they would be back in a while.

His mom came down the stairs, looked at the two of them, and asked, "Everything ok?"

"Everything's fine, Pixie." His dad whispered something in his mom's ear. The tips of that same ear turned beet-red as she tried to continue to look dignified. "See you in a bit," his dad said to his mom before grabbing his jacket from the peg near the door and tossing Kyle's to him.

"You bet I will," she replied with a wink. It was Kyle's turn to look embarrassed.

"If you two are through, can we go now?"

Warren laughed as they walked out to the car.

They drove down to the beach. It was cold and windy, so pretty much just the locals who lived nearby were moving around. They parked at one of the hotels on the beach. It was where his dad's favorite bar was located.

"Hi, Warren, how's the grandbaby?" one of the waitresses asked when they walked in. Kyle wondered how the woman knew about Cadence.

"Getting bigger every day."

"This is your son, Kyle, right?"

"Yep," Warren responded. They sat at a table by the window, giving them a good view of the boardwalk.

"Your daughter is the cutest thing."

"Thanks," Kyle said, unable to stop the smile spreading across his face.

"She has your eyes." He just smiled again and nodded.

"I'll be back in a moment," she said, before walking off.

"How does that woman know you have a granddaughter?"

"It's what grandparents do. They show off their grandchildren. Plus, the whole crew gave us a grand baby shower when we brought her home."

"What? Really?"

"Sure. Everyone here knows about Cadence." He pointed to the side of the cash register at the bar. "See, there's her picture up there."

Kyle just laughed. Sure enough, his daughter's picture was plastered on the cash register. He just shook his head.

The waitress came back, took their drink orders, and promised to bring out a plate of the Mountain High Nachos.

"Don't tell your mom about the nachos." Warren leaned in to tell his son. "She has us on this damn diet again."

"Then why are you eating the nachos?"

"It's tradition." He shrugged. "I always get them."

"Is that why you wanted to take a ride? So, you can secretly eat nachos away from mom?"

"I wanted to show you something."

"What?"

"See that bench over there?" Warren pointed to a bench on the boardwalk facing the water.

"Yes, what about it?"

"That's the bench where I saw my girlfriend kissing Brett Franklin."

Kyle looked at the bench again and then back at his dad. "Is this when you tell me you were eventually glad you saw them, otherwise you wouldn't have met mom."

Kyle looked around the restaurant. There weren't many people there, which was typical for the beach this time of year. This particular restaurant and bar catered to locals by having the same hours year-round.

"It was your mom on that bench kissing Brett Franklin." Kyle turned back to his dad. His face was passive, but he knew his dad was remembering that moment.

"Mom?"

227

Warren didn't reply. Kyle wondered what happened, not really wanting to know. No one wants to think of their parents as real people with real problems like everyone else.

Not taking his eyes from the bench, his dad spoke. "I'd come out to get a beaded bracelet she'd eyed the last time we took a walk out here. Of course, I knew she used to have a thing for Brett, but still, I pretended I had her whole heart at the time."

"Pretended?"

His dad looked at him. "Son, sometimes you want something so badly that you pretend a whole lot of things." He looked back at the bench, and Kyle followed his gaze, feeling the pain his dad must have felt. "I pretended your mom was over Brett just because she said she was." He paused again. "They'd been together all through high school. She found out that he'd been keeping time with Sue Lynn Moore, halfway through our senior year. They broke up. I'd had a crush on Pixie since sophomore year and jumped at the chance to ask her out. She said yes, of course, and I pretended it was because she liked me and not because she wanted to get back at Brett. We went on a few dates. I was so taken with her that I ignored the fact that she never seemed completely happy."

"How long did you go on like that?"

228

His dad gave a bitter chuckle. "Until the day I saw her on that bench."

"What did you say when you confronted her."

"I didn't."

"What do you mean, you didn't?"

"I never said a word about seeing her."

Kyle was confused. "Dad why are you telling me all of this?"

Warren went on, ignoring the question. "We had a date that night. I thought she would have canceled, but when I showed up, she was ready to go. We were driving up to Jacksonville to meet some friends at the drive-in."

The nachos arrived, and both men jumped in with both hands. Between bites, Kyle asked, "How could you just go on like you'd never seen that?"

"It made me pay more attention to her. She was polite on the date and said all the right things, but I knew her heart was somewhere else. Even though Brett was still seeing Sue Lynn, he didn't like the fact that Pixie was going out with me.

"I could tell that she was preoccupied on the date, but I was still as attentive as always. When I brought her home, I walked her to the door, but before I left I said, 'I've had a crush on you for the past two years. It has nothing to do with how beautiful you are

229

but everything to do with how beautiful you make others feel.'"

Kyle's brows knitted together. "What did you mean by that?"

Warren smiled. "She asked me the same thing."

"What did you say?"

"I told her that my favorite thing about her was how she never excluded people just because others did. I'd seen her sit with the kid who would normally eat alone. I'd watched her at the grocery store where I'd worked, helping the elderly get their groceries to the car or reach something on the shelf. I told her that I was crazy about her big heart because I wanted to be as loving and giving as she was."

"Mom's still like that," Kyle said.

"Yes, she is. But I didn't want to be the rebound guy, nor did I want to be a charity project."

"I can understand that. But, what does any of this have to do with me?"

"Anyway…I told Pixie that I would be leaving to go to college soon, and I knew that she would be as well. And after I told her about her beauty, I said, 'I just want you to be happy, Pixie. Even if that's not with me. You deserve happiness in your life, and I want that for you. I've enjoyed hanging out with you these past few months. Let me know when or if you'd like to go out again.'" Warren looked directly at Kyle. "I loved your mom, even then, but I wanted her to be happy. If that wasn't with me, then I was fine with that."

"How long did it take for her to come to her senses?"

"Longer than I wanted it to." He laughed. "Halfway through my first semester in Gainesville, I got a call telling me I had a visitor in the dorm. When I went down, thinking it was Evelyn from my study group, it turned out to be your mom."

Why hadn't Kyle ever heard this story before? Over the years, his dad told him tons of stories from his youth about him and his mom, but never this one.

"What did she want?" Considering the outcome, he could figure it out, but he wanted to hear it.

"She came to tell me that she was pregnant."

That bit of information, sure as hell wasn't what Kyle expected to hear. He sat up wide-eyed. Eventually a tiny question croaked from his throat, "What?"

"Yeah, that was my reaction as well." Kyle's mind was swimming with questions. "Just let me explain, son, before you jump to conclusions." Kyle's heart raced. He had no idea what his dad was about to tell him.

"Had you and mom slept together?" He cringed inside just to ask the question, but he had to know.

"No. Plus I hadn't seen her in a couple months."

"Who was she pregnant by? That Brett guy?" Being the only child, Kyle's senses was on high alert. He signaled for the waitress to bring them another round.

"Yes, she'd gone back to Brett."

Anger at his mom and sympathy for his dad collided with each other inside of Kyle. "Did he leave her when she told him she was pregnant?" he spat, not really sure who he was angry with—his mom, Brett, or his dad for not telling him about this. And why now? Why was his dad telling him this?

"No, in fact, he'd asked her to marry him." Kyle was floored again. "Yeah…" his dad said with a look of astonishment. "We took a walk outside at this bit of news.

"She turned to me and said, 'I thought I knew what I wanted until you showed me something real. I went back to Brett because he was familiar, and we'd been together forever…but those few dates with you, I could be myself without feeling like I was being judged.'

"I asked her what all this meant, and she said, 'It means I'm not happy with Brett. I've missed you, and I'm pregnant.'"

"Dad? What did you say to that?"

"The only thing I could say. I said 'Ok.'"

Kyle realized the baby she was pregnant with could not have been him. "What about the baby? What happened to it?" He knew his parents were both against abortion now, but he didn't know what their thoughts were at that age.

"Your mom got really sick a few weeks later and lost the baby. We were both very upset about it. I knew it wasn't my baby, but I loved it because it was a part of your mother." Warren took a long swig of beer, looked at the bench, and turned to Kyle. "I told you this story, son, because you can't drive yourself crazy wondering if Symphony is going to go back to Terry. She either wants to be with you or she doesn't. But, by no means am I saying you should just push her away. Let her know how you feel, and from there, it's up to her."

"Symphony knows I love her."

"Does she know you love her enough to let her choose someone else?"

Kyle thought about that. "Could you have really been ok with mom choosing another dude?"

"I'm not saying it wouldn't have torn me up inside. Hell, it did. But how happy can you be with someone who is always wondering 'what if' about someone else?"

Kyle sighed heavily. "You're right." He didn't want to imagine Symphony with Terry or anyone else, but he knew that if he knew she was just with him because of Cadence, it would eat a hole in their relationship… and in him.

Chapter Twenty-Seven

The airport was crowded, and her flight had been delayed twice already. Her morning flight was quickly turning into an evening one. She'd already had breakfast and lunch at the airport and hoped she didn't have to be there long enough to have dinner too.

She sat for a while at the gate, just watching people walk by—some ran to their gates. She watched a little girl struggle to pull her hot pink suitcase, refusing to let her dad or mom help. After she'd gotten it steady again and easy to roll, she looked up at her dad with a triumphant smile.

Symphony thought of Cadence. Like Terry, she too, wanted a family. She wanted to be happy and settled. Or rather, she wanted to start building something with someone. Her business, her life.

Symphony took the time to review some of the information Ethan had given her. She became restless again. It seemed like forever since she last saw Cadence. All she wanted to do was hold her baby. Expanding her business right now may be a crazy idea, but the time was right for it. She wasn't sure if it was serendipity or what, but things were falling into place too perfectly for her to ignore this opportunity.

Symphony slid the paperwork into her satchel and wondered what Ian would think about it. The conference turned out to be more beneficial than she'd anticipated. If she could get Ricco to step up to the plate, things would be perfect.

"Symphony!"

Symphony turned to see Ricco approaching, as if she'd conjured her up. When she was closer, she asked, "What're you doing here? I thought you left yesterday morning."

"Well…"

Symphony cocked an eye at Ricco. She was glowing. She looked around and saw no empty seats. Symphony grabbed her satchel. "Oh, no ma'am, I need to hear this." She led Ricco to a nearby restaurant and a couple seats tucked in the corner. "Spill it!" she insisted.

"Who are you, and what did you do with my boss? Because the woman I see before me asking personal questions is not the Symphony James I know."

Symphony gave her a pointed look.

Ok, maybe Ricco had a point. Before the trip, she and Ricco hardly ever talked about anything beyond work. She didn't care. She was starting a new chapter in her life, and damn it, she was a new Symphony James—the Symphony who knew exactly what she wanted and planned on getting it. She thought of Terry and smiled. He'd made her realize that the heart makes its own choices.

A waitress brought over a couple glasses of water and menus. They declined the menus but asked for an order of chips and salsa.

"You're asking me all my business…so, what's that look on your face?" Ricco demanded.

"That's the look of finally knowing what I want."

"And what's that?"

"I've decided to open a bakery in the neighborhood where Terry's company is revitalizing." Symphony decided to go with a safer explanation.

"What?"

"Yes. My friend Alex has been after me to do it for a while. And it just feels right."

"How're you going to run two shops in two states?"

"I plan on having great people on my team to run them for me." Symphony waved her hands in front of Ricco. "We'll get back to that. Tell me why you didn't leave yesterday."

Ricco bit her lip and put her head down.

"Let me guess. You were with Kenny?"

"Yes," she acquiesced softly.

"You two must've hit it off."

"We did."

"Are you planning on continuing to see each other?"

"We know it's pretty impossible to maintain a long distance…whatever this is."

"It's not impossible."

"What about you and Terry? You seemed to have more going on than being just friends from college. Was he your boyfriend?"

"Yes."

"Was it serious?"

"Yes."

"What happened?"

"Me."

"Huh?"

"I broke up with him right before we were about to graduate."

"Why?"

"Fear."

Symphony waited for Ricco to grill her about that, but she just nodded her head as if she understood completely. She gave Ricco an appraising look. "Ricco, do you think we can be friends?"

"Oh, after this trip, you thought you had a choice?"

A choice?

A choice.

All this time she thought she had a choice to make. Being with Terry yesterday made her realize that she'd been thinking way too hard about all of this. Life was full of choices—some good, some mistakes—and Symphony was determined not to make the same one twice.

"Symphony?"

With a huge smile on her face, she reached a hand across the table to shake on their new friendship. "I'm glad to call you my friend, Naricco Maki."

"So, now that we're officially friends, did you know that Ian and Marylyn used to have a thing?" Ricco asked.

"Whatever they had or didn't have, I don't want to know about it." Symphony sure as hell didn't want to know any of the shop gossip. Especially if it had anything to do with her employees fooling around. "Besides, he's married now." Ricco choked on a chip she'd just shoved in her mouth. "Damn girl, I didn't mean to kill you with the news."

A few people looked over at them until Ricco's coughs subsided. She took a sip of water. The waitress came over.

"You ok, ma'am?"

"No." The word was hoarse and barely audible. She tried clearing her throat and spoke again. "But I'll survive. So glad to know that my friend here, is so concerned." She pointed at Symphony.

Symphony was about to choke now, laughing at Ricco's reaction to the news she'd found just as shocking. A lady stopped by the table.

"Lift your arms, dear."

Ricco waved the woman away. "Thanks, I'm fine. It just went down the wrong way. My friend just told me she was gay."

Water shot out of Symphony's mouth as the woman raised a brow and walked away from the table. After a few steps, the lady turned to look at Symphony. *Well, damn. Hasn't she ever seen a gay woman before?* Symphony thought, trying not to say something ugly to the her. "You should be ashamed of yourself for telling that woman that."

"Well, I'm not. She should be ashamed for that look she gave you." She took another sip of water and took in a few deep breaths. "Now, what're you talking about? Ian is married?"

"Yeah, that's why he couldn't come to the conference."

"Get out of here!"

"He flew to Hawaii to get married and had plans on being at work tomorrow." Symphony wiped up the rest of the water she'd spit out on the table. "I told him I didn't want to see him for at least two weeks."

"I'm sure Marylyn is devastated. From what I heard, she was crazy about Ian."

"As long as it doesn't interfere with what's going on at Symphony's, that's their business."

"Not to take advantage of our friendship or anything, but do you think I can showcase a feature every now and then?" Before Symphony could answer, she continued, "I mean, of course I'd run it by you first."

"I don't mean to take advantage of our friendship, but do you think you can run an entire store?"

Ricco choked on another chip.

Chapter Twenty-Eight

It was dark by the time she landed in Jacksonville. She'd called Pixie before she left the airport to let her know she would be home soon. Even now, Symphony was still shocked that she was a mom. It wasn't the first time she'd been away from her daughter. She was with her grandparents and dad often, but it was her first time going out of town and being so far away from Cadence. She pulled into her garage, not really feeling like unloading all her luggage, but did it anyway.

Taking advantage of the opportunity to shower and wash her hair without having to worry about listening for the baby, Symphony closed herself in the bathroom and got the water as hot as she could stand it. Afterward, she wrapped her hair in a towel and slipped into a pair of Disney sleep pants and a T-shirt. She relaxed in her favorite chair with a mug of hot chocolate.

The past few days were a whirlwind. The conference was such a success on so many levels. There were new business contacts, people begging her to expand her business, and the actual prospect of opening a new store in Boston, which would allow her to partner with Alex's restaurant there. She'd already started shipping breads and desserts to Alex's restaurant in New Orleans, as well as several others in Florida and Georgia. Soon, she would have to open a centralized production kitchen to keep up with the restaurant requests.

Then there was Terry.

Terry Phoenix. A lifetime of memories flooded her, which brought a soft smile to her lips.

Terry wanted to give her everything she'd wanted when they first met. For years, she'd thought she'd lost her opportunity for happiness with him. Being with him yesterday had been so natural and familiar.

Symphony heard a car drive up and went to the window, verifying it was one of the Deans bringing Cadence home. By the time she got to the door and opened it, Kyle was unsnapping Cadence from the car seat.

"Need any help?" she yelled out. She still had the towel wrapped around her head.

"I got her. Go back inside if your hair is wet." The night air was cold and windy.

Symphony ducked back just inside the door, anxious to hold Cadence. Kyle walked in holding their smiling baby. Cadence reached out for her mom and immediately started grabbing at the towel. "You're going to loosen it, Cay." Cadence giggled sweetly when Symphony gave her a tight hug and kisses all over her plump cheeks. Kyle stood and watched just a moment before he went back to the car to get the rest of her stuff. Symphony watched him walk away. She still got the same flutter in her chest when he turned those blue eyes on her.

"Do you want this stuff here or in her room?" Kyle asked when he returned to the house.

"If you don't mind, put it in her room, please."

When he hadn't come out right away, she asked, "What're you doing?"

"I'm putting her stuff away. I'm sure you're exhausted," he called out. "And she's already had her bath."

Kyle was such a great dad and did everything he could to make things easier for Symphony. It didn't take him long to put the baby's clothes and toys away. He walked into the family room, and Cadence reached for him. He pulled her into his arms and sang a little song to her. Cadence sang along with her usual singsong "da-da-da-da…" She was such a happy baby.

"You can sit there," Symphony said, pointing to the sofa. "Would you like some loaded hot chocolate?"

His eyes lit and sparkled like sapphires in the sun. "Sure, that'll be great."

She chuckled on her way to the kitchen, thinking about Kyle's sweet tooth. He loved her hot chocolate. She used special cocoa, milk, real whipping cream for the topping, along with marshmallows, chocolate chips, a dash of cinnamon, and a squirt of caramel.

Halfway through the hot chocolate, Cadence was sound asleep. They both put her to bed before going back out to the family room to finish their cocoa. She refilled both their cups. An awkward silence fell over them as she warmed her hands on the mug.

"Your trip go ok?"

"Yes. I'll need to go back after Christmas. I'm going to open another Symphony's there."

Kyle's face was expressionless, but his eyes held hers. She knew exactly what his was thinking. "Are you moving there?" he asked.

"No. I would never move Cadence away from you like that without at least discussing it with you first."

"But you'll have to spend a lot of time there." It wasn't a question.

Symphony didn't answer. She just looked at him. The space between them grew, even though neither moved.

She didn't know how to tell him. She was afraid of his reaction.

Symphony got up, placed her mug on her kitchen counter, took a deep breath, and returned to the family room. She did not sit. Instead, she stood behind the chair she'd just vacated, needing a barrier between them.

"I kissed him." Her words came out in a rush.

She watched an unfamiliar expression cross his face briefly before it became guarded.

His eyes fell to the floor—head nodding. "Terry." Kyle's voice was distant and resigned. She stood there waiting for him to say something more, to yell, to do something. After several minutes, she couldn't stand it.

"I kissed Terry," she began.

"You said that already." His eyes were still on the floor.

"Yeah, well…I realized something."

He looked up at her then. His eyes no longer held the sparkle they had when he first arrived. Her gut twisted, knowing her words were hurting him.

"What Symphony? What did you realize?"

She walked around the chair to sit in it and face him. "Terry and I have a past." Her fingers twisted in her lap. "He's familiar, and it was very easy to pretend that there was not a time when we were apart."

"But there was. There was a time when you were apart."

"Yes."

"Are you willing to forget about what we shared to live in the past with Terry?"

"That's just it. I don't want to live in the past."

"What do you mean?" His words were guarded.

"I'm trying to say that the past is the past…my present nor my future is with Terry. That's over."

It was true. She knew now that the memories of times with Terry had haunted her because of the way they'd ended. She hadn't had any closure with him. Maybe she was afraid of allowing him to love her at the time, but that time was gone. Life moved on.

She truly enjoyed spending time with Terry. He was fun and indulged her every whim. It was difficult not to be drawn to a man who paid attention to her and let her have her way. However, after a while, she knew that would not appeal to her. She knew she needed someone who would give her a kick in the ass when she needed it. She knew she needed someone to set her straight sometimes.

You're my dream girl.

He'd said it so many times, but it was that last time—standing in her hotel room in his arms—that she really understood how serious he was. It wasn't a frivolous, cutesy statement. He truly believed it. Terry was in love with a ghost, an idea—not her. His fatalistic beliefs were so ingrained in him that it didn't matter what she'd done, who she'd become, or if she still loved him. He believed they were destined to be together and that everything would work itself out.

Well, she had news for him. It was because of what she'd done, who she'd become, and who she'd loved since him that made her who she was today.

And that girl was not the one Terry had met in the college library.

It was impossible for her to regret any decisions she'd made along the way. Those were the choices that shaped her life as it was now.

"We were in my hotel room last night," she began.

"Symphony, I really don't want to hear this."

"Please, Kyle." She sat next to him on the sofa. "I want you to understand."

He closed his eyes briefly, as if steeling himself for her words. He sighed and gave her a nearly imperceptible nod.

"We'd been shopping and exploring all day and had a great time. He insisted on walking me up to my room. One thing led to another, and I was in his arms. I hadn't been touched in so long, so…" Kyle made a noise akin to a groan.

"Will you get to the point?" he gritted through clinched teeth.

"Well, we started kissing, and then he put his hands under my shirt…"

Kyle made a move to stand, but Symphony placed a hand on his thigh.

"Please, Kyle. I don't want there to be any secrets between us."

He looked into her eyes and the pain reflected in his, nearly broke her heart.

"The moment his hands touched me…I knew…I knew they didn't belong there." It was Symphony who stood then. She took a couple of steps and stood behind the chair again. "I jumped away from him as if he'd burned me." She wanted Kyle to understand that Terry was not a threat to them. She hadn't realized she was crying or that Kyle was standing in front of her until his thumb brushed away some of the wetness from her face.

"It's ok, babe," He crooned as he pulled her into his arms. "Everything's going to be ok…We're going to be ok."

"I'd let him in your space, Kyle, and it tore me up inside."

Kyle cocked is head to the side with a questioning brow, and Symphony realized how that last statement sounded. "No…not like that. It was just a kiss…that was escalating. But that's all!" She took a deep breath. "I'm sorry, for everything."

"You have nothing to be sorry for, Symphony. Life happens. Neither of ours were ideal, but we kept moving forward anyway."

Kyle put his hands on hers. They were more than familiar. His hands belonged.

"So now what?" she asked.

"Do you love me, Symphony James?"

"Yes."

"And I love you."

"I'm glad, but now what?" Cadence's soft cries rose from the baby monitor on the coffee table.

"Now, we go check on our little girl."

Chapter Twenty-Nine

"So, things are back on with you and Symphony, eh?" Warren Dean asked his son.

"What makes you say that?" Kyle asked as he set up the lighting for some food shots he had scheduled for Symphony's new website.

"Don't you think I know my own son?"

"Yeah, well, things are better. She's going to open a bakery in Boston."

Warren picked up a camera, looked through the view finder, and placed it back on the table. Kyle watched him. He knew his dad missed working full-time. "Doesn't most of the Phoenix family live in Boston?"

"Yes, Dad."

"Terry Phoenix?"

He still felt a tightening in his gut just thinking about that dude. She'd admitted to kissing him. Just thinking about another man's mouth and hands on his Symphony—

"Son?"

"Yes."

"And you're not worried?"

251

"Nope. An old man had a really long talk with me about a bench." He would be lying to himself if he didn't wish she weren't going to open another Symphony's in Boston, but if they were going to work, he had to trust her. And he desperately wanted them to work. He hated leaving her and Cadence to go back home to Daytona every night. That hour drive was starting to wear on him. Not to mention, he wanted them to truly be a family.

"Old man, huh? I'll show you an old man!" Warren took Kyle by surprise when he grabbed him in a headlock and rubbed his knuckles against the top of his head until Kyle started pleading for him to let go.

And that's how Symphony found them.

"Am I interrupting.?"

Both men looked up at her in the doorway of the studio. Kyle was grateful when his dad let go of his neck. He'd spotted his granddaughter in the stroller, and she immediately reached for him. Kyle held Symphony's eyes for several moments before they both looked toward their daughter and her grandfather.

Warren unbuckled Cadence from the seat and held her high in the air. "How's my best girl?" he asked her.

Kyle watched his dad. Cadence turned him into someone he'd not met before. He'd never been unkind or very hard on him, but he'd not been emotional either. Since Cadence was born, his dad talked to him more, told him he loved him, and gave him relationship advice. He chuckled to himself, walked over to Symphony, and gave her a soft kiss on her lips.

"Hey, babe." The kiss and endearment were new since their talk the other night. Not much else had changed in their relationship.

"Hello. Looks like you two are having a great time," Symphony said, not trying too hard to suppress a chuckle.

Kyle tried to get a kiss from his little girl too, but she was too enamored with her Pop-Pop. He loved seeing his dad so light and happy.

"I was just trying to remind my son who was the boss." He bounced Cadence in his arms. "What do we owe the pleasure to have you two beauties here?"

"I'm bringing the pastries for the photoshoot."

"Photoshoot?" Warren asked her.

"I'm taking photos of Symphony's pastries for her website, Dad," Kyle answered for her.

"Did Kyle tell you I'm opening another bakery in Boston?"

"He sure did. Congratulations! That's pretty exciting. Must mean your business is doing really well."

Kyle could tell Symphony was slightly embarrassed by the comment. He knew that she was more successful than some of the more popular chains in the area, but she definitely didn't boast about it. Her pastries were so sought after that Alex was willing to pay the exorbitant shipping costs to have Symphony's baked goods trucked from Florida to Louisiana. The first time he'd seen the refrigerated truck with the Symphony's logo on it, the pride he felt for her almost overwhelmed him.

"I guess it is pretty exciting. I'm still in the very early stages of everything. Trying to plan out who, what, and where. I have another meeting after Christmas." She turned to Kyle. "Will you be over tomorrow tonight? I want to finally put up the Christmas tree for Cadence."

Of course, he would be there. He was surprised she felt the need to ask.

"Symphony, I'm glad you stopped by. My sister, Beverly, is in town for a couple days. Do you mind if I bring Cadence over to the house to visit with her? She's dying to meet her."

Symphony looked at Kyle. He gave her a shrug. "You two can pick her up when you're done here," Warren added.

"Sure," Symphony agreed.

Warren put Cadence back in the stroller and gave Symphony a huge bear-hug.

"Hey…Hey! Go hug on your own girl!" Kyle told his dad. Kyle picked up Cadence and held her before her grandfather whisked her away. He could tell she'd just had a bath. She smelled like heaven. Kyle buried his face in her neck and his heart melted from the sweet chortles that were against his ears.

It didn't take long for his dad to escape with Cadence before he and Symphony changed their minds about allowing their daughter to go off for a while with her grandfather. All their cars had a seat for her, and all their homes had everything she would need. Their family was small, but his daughter was loved. And just to think, someone tried to take her away from them. His chest tightened every time he thought about it.

This was the first time he photographed food, and Kyle found that it wasn't as easy as it seemed. It took several adjustments with his camera and the lighting for him to finally get the perfect shot he was looking for.

"We could have been done a couple hours ago," Symphony said as he devoured his favorite lemon pastries in a couple bites. He loved that she always brought him something special. Either something she wanted him to try or one that she knew he loved.

"Yes," he said around the food in his mouth, "but do you want good pictures are great ones?" He licked a finger, so thankful that his girl was the best baker in the world.

She tossed a crumpled napkin at him. "Use a napkin, you slob."

He caught it easily and tossed it aside. "And waste food? No way!"

Kyle changed his lens on the camera and looked up at Symphony. Since she'd taken off her jacket, he had a difficult time focusing on the job and not her. Now that the job was over, she was all he could see.

Her fluffy pink sweater fell in such a way that exposed her left shoulder. From the window, the sun fell on her, highlighting the golden strands in her auburn curls that tumbled just past that exposed shoulder. It was her haunted beauty that'd captured him so long ago and kept him up night after night when he had no idea where she was. But today, at this very moment, her beauty took him so by surprise he couldn't breathe.

Symphony looked out the window. She either had something on her mind or there was something out there that had her attention.

When air finally forced from his lungs and through his mouth, he worried about disturbing the moment. Her face was so earnest and thoughtful, with just a hint of sadness, he wondered what was on her mind. It was in moments like this that she seemed out of his reach—just beyond his grasp. It was in moments like this that the hurts of her past seem to engulf her like a blanket. The moments when he wanted to hold her, protect her, and love her with all his might.

Picking up the camera, he framed her in the viewfinder and started snapping. Symphony turned at the sound of the clicks.

"What're you doing?"

He loved that she didn't cover her face and shy away from the camera. Instead, she cocked her head to the side and faced him. The clicking of the camera echoed in his ears as she took steps toward him—her stride, careful, determined, and a little mischievous.

He absolutely, without a shadow of a doubt, loved Symphony Blaire James. He didn't ever want to live another day without her in his life. Not just as the mother of his daughter but as his partner for life, his love, his life. He was about to put the camera down and voice his thoughts when she stopped and pulled the sweater over her head.

He was no fool.

The camera still to his eye, he clicked away. Thank God, they'd locked the studio doors behind his dad, but the look in her hazel eyes told him that she didn't give one royal damn if the doors were locked or not.

She tossed the sweater when she was about halfway between the wall and him and slid her black leggings down to the floor. Stepping out of them, she kicked them out of her path.

Kyle's hands shook, though he still tried to steady the camera. He wanted to wipe the perspiration that was forming on his forehead, but he didn't dare do anything that would disturb the moment.

Symphony filled his lens, clad in a black half-bra and pink and black panties. Her skin, a golden glow that filled his studio. She was perfect. Her face no longer shadowed with sadness or fixed in concentration. It held something that he hadn't seen reflected from her in quite some time.

Trust.

She trusted him.

Every confident step, the bold way she held him captive, every moment she stood in front of his camera let him know, she trusted him.

Kyle suddenly realized she was there. Her face filling his lens. He still held the camera, looking at her through it, but she was no longer the subject. He was. She looked through the camera at his soul, and his soul drank her up. He prayed that the look in her eyes was the promise he wished for.

Kyle clicked the camera one last time before sitting it on the table.

"Do you see me?" she asked.

"Yes."

More urgently, she asked again. "Do you see me?" It was a plea, but he didn't know for what.

"Yes, Symphony, I see you," he tried to reassure her.

"What do you see?" Her voice was barely above a whisper.

"My life."

Chapter Thirty

My life.

Those two words were everything.

She was his life.

That's what he saw when he looked at her.

Those two words were the perfect answer, because that's exactly what she saw when she looked at him. This man loved her; he was the father of her child; and she was his life. His life.

Symphony didn't want to spend another moment not building a life with him. She wanted this moment to be the first memory of their new time together.

The instant her lips touched his, her body took over the show. She felt him place her on the desk, and she knew before it was all over he would never look at that desk the same way again. Her legs captured him as they locked around his waist. Her eyes called him to her like a siren. She knew she had more than his body. She had his attention—his heart.

Her breath caught, knowing that his whole heart was hers to have and care for. Kyle looked down at her, and she found herself so lost in his penetrating blue eyes that she didn't even realize her panties were gone until she saw him rip open the condom wrapper and felt his heat pressed against her.

She was ready.

This was the moment she'd waited for. This was the moment she'd dreamed about, even when her conscious thoughts couldn't remember him. This was her choice. Kyle Dean was the man she chose to surrender her heart to. She wanted this man and no other—to connect their bodies and make them one.

Her eyes slid closed in sweet anticipation.

"Look at me," his voice sensually commanded. "I want to see all of you when I make you forever mine."

She could have come at that very instant. His bold statement, made with a control she could tell he could barely contain, was nearly her undoing.

His name tore from her lips as he entered her. His sweet heat was so delicious, she couldn't keep her eyes open past the first stroke. He filled her over and over, branding her his forever.

Forever.

The phone rang.

Symphony was startled out of her memories of the day before. She placed the box of ornaments on the table and reached for the phone.

261

"Hey there," she said, answering cheerfully.

"Hey." The sound of Kyle's voice had her eyes slipping closed and her hands tightening on the phone.

"Hey," she said again. She couldn't help the smile on her face. She felt like a teenager, talking to the boy she'd always had a crush on.

"Should I plan to stay when I come over for tree decorating."

"Stay forever," Symphony heard herself say.

Silence answered her. She looked to see if she'd lost the connection.

"Be careful what you ask for," she thought she heard him say, but the words were so low that she wasn't quite sure. "Will there be hot chocolate?"

"Of course."

"Would you like for me to bring dinner?" Kyle asked, though her mind was still on what she thought she heard.

"Sure. Surprise me with something good."

"Oh, I'll definitely have something good."

She giggled again. "We'll see you tonight.

Kyle arrived with spaghetti and meatballs, courtesy of Pixie and Warren. Pixie's famous secret sauce and Warren's specialty meatballs. Symphony was sure Kyle's parents were feeding the spaghetti to

Cadence, because the moment she saw it on the table, she pushed aside her baby food and reached for the spaghetti with her mouth open. Symphony looked at Kyle. Kyle mashed a tiny bit on his plate and fed it to her. Cadence smacked loudly and opened her mouth for more. Yep. She'd definitely had it before.

After dinner, Symphony fell into her big comfy chair. "I'm stuffed. Whose idea was it to put the tree up tonight?"

"That would be you, ma'am."

"That's what I was afraid of." They both watched Cadence scoot along the floor, trying to get to the ornaments by the tree.

"Will you marry me?" The words sprang from her lips.

Kyle was picking up Cadence when her words finally reached him. She'd known that night in the hotel room with Terry that her life was with Kyle. Kyle either wanted the same, or he didn't.

He stood with Cadence in his arms, walked to the sofa, and sat—never taking his eyes off her.

Could she have been wrong in assuming they wanted the same thing? He stared at her so long, she wanted to take the words back—to save face. But they were out there now, and she wanted him to know where she stood.

"Kyle I…" Embarrassment heated her cheeks.

"Don't you dare," he said sharply.

She was pretty sure her face was turning red. "What?"

"Don't you dare try to take that back." Kyle walked over and placed Cadence in the bouncy chair she loved. When he returned, he sat on the coffee table directly in front of her and took her hands in his. "I can tell by your face that you've misunderstood my silence."

"Yeah?"

"Yeah."

"Well, I still don't have an answer."

"Well…you kind of stole my Christmas present."

"Huh?"

"I was going to ask you to marry me on Christmas day."

"You were?"

"Yes.'"

"So, what are you saying?"

"Yes."

"Yes, you'll marry me?" she asked. Just making sure.

"Yes," he responded, right before he pulled her to him for a kiss.

After a few moments, she broke off the kiss. "Will you marry me tomorrow?"

"What?"

"Tomorrow? Will you marry me tomorrow, or as soon as it can be arranged?" Before he could answer, she rushed on. "Tonight, after we put up the tree, I want to take our first family picture, and on Christmas, I want us to truly be a family. The Deans. I don't want to wait another day to be yours."

"Baby, you've been mine since that day you put a spell on me in the airport." They both smiled. "Don't you want a big wedding…the works?" he asked, his tone serious.

"I have everything I want right here in this room."

Kyle's eyes studied her, and his face became serious. "Are you sure this is what you want, Symphony? Are you sure I'm who you want to spend the rest of your life with? This is a huge decision."

Symphony knew exactly what he was asking her and why. He wanted to know if Terry Phoenix was out of her system.

"I'm absolutely sure that you love me. I'm absolutely sure that I've loved you since you showed up at my aunt's funeral. I'm positive that I've never stopped loving you, even when my brain was broken, and I couldn't remember you." She squeezed his hands, willing him to believe her. "I love you, Kyle Dean, and I want to spend the rest of my life showing you just how much. Yes, I'm sure I want to marry you."

"Symphony James, I'll marry you tonight if that were possible."

She hugged him tightly, not able to stop the tears spilling from her eyes. "Unfortunately, we have to get a license and wait three days."

"That long?" he teased her before pulling her to her feet and wiping her tears. Kyle held her.

"Do you feel my arms?" he asked.

"Yes," she replied, nodding.

"They are a promise that I will always protect you. My heartbeat is my promise that for as long as it beats, I will love you." He tilted her chin up and captured her lips. When the kiss was done, he said, "My kisses are my promise to be faithful and loyal to you, my love, my life, my wife."

His wife. Her heart sang. And when she thought he couldn't possibly say anything sweeter, he whispered next to her ear, "My body is yours, and even if it may no longer be able, I will provide for you and our children." She cried. Never had she felt so loved.

She was so sure of his feelings for her that all the fears and doubts she'd harbored no longer existed.

But he wasn't done.

"Symphony, I promise to never be the cause of your sadness, and when you are sad, I want to be the reason it goes away."

She couldn't speak. How could she? This beautiful, honorable, strong, talented man loved her with his entire being. All she could do was hold on to him—her promise to love him back.

Chapter Thirty-One

"What happened to our quiet, quickie wedding?" Kyle asked his wife.

"Alex and Pixie happened," she replied.

It all started with her phone call to Alex.

No, she could not get married in a courthouse. No, it could not take place in three days. No, it would not be small and quiet with only his parents and Cadence.

"First of all, whether you accept it or not, I am your best friend, and by default, because she is mine, that makes Candice your best friend too…and as your best friends, we must be there!"

Symphony rolled her eyes but couldn't help the smile that turned up her lips. She knew it was no use to be adamant about her own plans. Alex was going to interject her way into this somehow.

"What do you have in mind, Alex? And keep in mind that I want to be married before Christmas."

"A sunset wedding off the South Carolina coast on Christmas Eve sounds absolutely perfect to me."

Symphony had to admit that it sounded absolutely perfect to her as well. And thus, the frenzy began. There were guests to invite, finding a place for them to stay, a dress to buy, a caterer to hire on such short notice, and so many other things that Symphony's head started to spin. Luckily, Alex and Candice took on all the details except the dress.

Ricco was ecstatic and insisted on baking and decorating the cake. Symphony was sure Gloria Phoenix would allow Ricco to take over her kitchen for the occasion of baking a wedding cake, so Ricco could keep it a secret until the reception. Alex offered the use of their yacht, *The Phoenix*, for the ceremony, but Symphony declined. She had not yet gotten over her negative experience from the evening of Ethan and Sophia's reception, when she was nearly assaulted by that bastard Cooper Read, who was trying to blackmail her and steal her recipes.

Her dress had not been as much of a chore as she'd expected. Ricco took her to a vintage wedding boutique in Jacksonville, the very afternoon she was told about the impending wedding of her new friend. The first dress she tried on was so perfect she didn't need nor want to look further.

The dress was made of a beautiful white taffeta. It had an off-the-shoulder neckline with long sleeves accented with thick velvet along the cuffs and an elegant standing collar. Symphony did not think she was the type of woman who wore a train on her gown, but when she saw the detachable cathedral train at the back of the dress, it was pure perfection. The new curves she'd earned from Cadence would look fabulous in the ensemble.

The evening of Christmas Eve was absolutely perfect. Deep rich red roses were everywhere. The pier was covered with them, and her beautiful bouquet were full of them except for one lone white rose in the center.

The weather was perfect. There was just a little chill in the air, but the sky was a clear indigo with a brilliant streak of orange running along the horizon. She loved that the home her aunt left her was on the western side of the island so she could see the sunset. She usually watched it from the porch swing, but today, she watched it in the reflection in her husband's eyes.

She did not hear the cheers of the two dozen or so guests who'd come to witness the declaration of love of two people whose love could not be denied. She could only hear that he vowed to love her until death do them part. The words filled her head. This man standing before her vowed to love her for the rest of his life, no matter what.

No matter what.

Even when times were hard, he would love her. He would love her when she was sick, when she was a mess, when she didn't love herself. This beautiful man had vowed to love her anyway. More than that, he would be by her side through it all.

When Reverend Slate declared them husband and wife, Symphony felt such an overwhelming sense of obligation to protect the heart of this man who had entrusted her with it so willingly, that tears filled her eyes.

Tears fell as he imprisoned her lips with his, sealing them to one another.

"No tears today, baby," he whispered next to her ear when he ended the kiss just before it became too inappropriate for an audience.

"I can't help it," she replied. "I love you so much."

His answering smile was like sunshine. She would never tire of seeing it. He kissed her again and scooped her into his arms before turning to the crowd.

Somewhere in the midst of the roar from the guests, Symphony heard Reverend Slate yell, "I present to you, Mr. and Mrs. Kyle James Dean!" As a coincidence, her name was now Symphony Blaire James Dean. They were made for each other.

The guests were all in the capable hands of Pixie, Alex, Candice, and Ricco on the beautiful grounds of what she would always consider her aunt's home. There were heaters spread around to provide light and keep everyone warm enough. Food, drinks, and the beautiful wedding cake were being consumed freely.

Most of the guests were staying at the home of Dixon and Gloria Phoenix on the other side of the island. Some of the guests were staying on Alex and Joshua's yacht or in Symphony's home. She and Kyle would be anchored out in the middle of the ocean on a rented yacht—a gift from Landon and Candice Phoenix. They would spend the night and return ashore for a huge Christmas brunch, after which the guests would depart to get home for Christmas dinner. In the case of the Phoenix family, they would go to Dixon and Gloria's side of the island for their family Christmas.

Of course, Terry was not there. Symphony was sure he knew she was getting married, but for obvious reasons, he had not been invited to the wedding.

"So, when do we get to leave?" Kyle asked, in between a few feathery kisses along her exposed collarbone. "We've had our first dance, cut the cake, and thrown the bouquet and garter. We've done our traditional wedding duties."

"Don't you want to mingle with our guests?"

"They aren't our guests. You're the only one I wanted to invite."

"Are we bad parents for not being with our daughter on Christmas Eve night?"

"Babe, she won't even remember this Christmas, and we'll be here with her in the morning to watch her try to open her presents." The pile of presents underneath the tree for Cadence was ridiculously large for a baby who was only seven months old.

Symphony turned to the small crowd of people with a small frown on her face. Kyle turned her face back to him, and the kiss he gave her was his promise that she would not regret leaving their reception.

They quickly said their goodbyes, checked on their now sleeping baby, and took the small boat to the yacht that was anchored a couple of miles from the island.

"Is *that* it?" Kyle asked, his tone filled with awe.

"I guess," she said, looking around. "Landon said it was called *Missy II*."

"*Missy II*?" he questioned. "I wonder what *Missy I*, looks like."

Before she could answer, two crewmen greeted them and quickly moored the small boat to the huge yacht. Symphony couldn't believe they would be spending a week surrounded by such lavishness. Another member of the crew gave them a quick tour of the place before directing them to the largest stateroom aboard. The room was larger than her bedroom in her house. There was a big sitting area, and even a balcony where they could have dinner if they wanted.

Two champagne-filled flutes along with a small buffet of finger foods and fruit awaited them on a beautiful glass table. She looked up at Kyle. He, too, was surprised by the generous gift from Landon and Candice.

"Wow!" They both exclaimed when they were left alone. At first, they were worried about their privacy when they'd been told there would be crewmen aboard, but neither no longer worried about that, considering the vastness of the vessel.

Kyle looked at the food and back down at her. "Hungry?"

"Sure I am." A slow smile spread across her face.

"Oh yeah? There's so many choices," he replied, returning her smile. "What would you like?"

"I would like a big ol' heaping of my husband…I've never had it before."

"A big ol' heaping, huh? What a great choice."

"Yes, Mr. Dean, you are."

"Well, Mrs. Dean, I think that can be arranged. May I help you out of your dress?"

"You may."

He unsnapped the thick velvet that lined her collar and shoulders. She turned her back to him and told him how to remove the train. She felt his lips along her neck to her shoulder and nearly melted into the floor.

"When I saw you walk out of the house," he said in between kisses, his voice husky and awe-filled, "I couldn't believe that you were walking to me and that I would be able to have you by my side for the rest of my life. The first time I saw you in the airport, I thought you were beautiful, but today, you were a vision. Beautiful seemed like such a small word to describe you, Symphony. I love you so much. I'm going to spend the rest of my life showing you. I promise to be a good husband."

Her husband. Kyle Dean was her husband—for better or for worse, he was hers.

Standing in the middle of the most extravagant room she'd ever seen, wearing white stockings, garters, and white lingerie, she wanted to let Mr. Dean know that his Mrs. Dean was going to spend the rest of the night setting the tone for their marriage bed.

With her dress pooled at her feet, Symphony turned to him and looked him up and down. "Mr. Dean, I do declare that you clean up well."

He smiled, and she wasted no time undressing him. When she'd completed the task, he wasted no time lifting her into his arms and placing her on the bed.

Kyle reached for the snaps on her garters, but she stopped him. "No, let me do the rest for you."

He kneeled, naked, at the side of the bed, and for the next few minutes she teased him with each snap of the garter, with the slow lazy slide each stocking took as it traveled down, first one leg and then the other. His eyes followed her fingers as they traced the lace around the cups of her bra before she released the front closer, her twin mounds springing free. The desire she saw in his gaze was almost tangible. Before she could reach to remove her panties, Kyle's mouth captured a hard nipple, and a spike of desire shot straight through her.

She'd wanted to slowly undress in front of him to drive him crazy, but he was taking another path, and it was all right with her. She was ready for him. While his mouth made love to one breast and then the other, his hands were trying hard not to rip her panties off. When she felt then slipping past her ankles, she also felt herself being moved farther into the bed.

Symphony's body trembled with wanting him.

"You cold?" he asked.

"No, I just want you."

"I'm yours, Symphony."

"For better or for worse," she repeated the vow, trying not to get emotional.

"Yes, Mrs. Dean, for better or for worse."

His mouth seemed to be everywhere at once. "Kyle…" she groaned, her need nearly choking her.

"I'm here, my wife." And there he was, filling her, loving her, truly making her his. Together, they created a symphony of their physical love. Over and over, their beautiful notes rose and fell—music they would make for the rest of their lives, together.

Epilogue

"Do you think she'll be ok on the plane?" Symphony asked Kyle for the hundredth time since they'd left home.

"Babe, she'll be fine."

"What about her ears? I just don't want to be thousands of feet in the air and have her crying for two and a half hours."

"Symphony, she'll be fine." Kyle picked up Cadence and bounced her on his lap. She smiled up at him as she always did. Symphony loved how Cadence was so crazy about her dad.

It didn't look like the flight would be crowded, so at least there was that. "You're just nervous about signing all the paperwork for the construction of your new store."

She had to admit that she was nervous about the new store. Not only was it a lot of money, but it was a huge undertaking, not to mention a huge risk.

They were traveling to Boston to meet with Ethan Phoenix about the new store. Joshua and Alex would surely take advantage of the situation to spoil Cadence rotten.

It turned out that Kyle was correct. Cadence had no issues on the flight, and everyone who sat around her, as well as all the flight attendants, fell in love with her.

After Cadence was settled with her godparents at their Boston home, where they all would stay during their visit, Kyle and Symphony headed to Phoenix Industries to meet with Ethan.

"How long do you think Alex and Joshua will be here in Boston?" Kyle asked.

"She told me they usually set sail on the *Phoenix*, sometime during spring."

"Where do they go?"

"Where ever they want, I guess."

"And she owns a sports bar and restaurant here and in New Orleans, as well as practice law?"

"She doesn't practice law that much anymore, but she does keep her licenses active. She's not very hands-on in the restaurant businesses either. She has a partner. Her former boss where she used to bartend. He runs the places, I guess."

Symphony could tell Kyle wanted to ask more questions, but he needed to listen to the directions from the GPS.

"Well, it looks like marriage is agreeing with the two of you," Ethan announced when they were escorted into his office by his office assistant. They both smiled up at him. Symphony was surprised to see Landon too. She hadn't realized that she would be meeting with them both, but she was glad to see him as well. They were greeted warmly—hugs all around. After all they'd done for Kyle and her, they felt like family. They would all be together at Alex's sports bar later, anyway.

"I didn't think we'd be seeing you until later tonight, Landon," Symphony stated, not hiding her surprise.

Everyone took a seat, Ethan behind his desk. Landon pulled a chair to sit near Symphony and Kyle.

"Well, normally, Ethan handles all the paperwork, but there were a few issues that came up."

"What kind of issues?" both Kyle and she asked.

"Many of the residents are worried about gentrification."

"Terry told Ricco that gentrification wouldn't be an issue."

Ethan stood and sat on the front edge of his desk. "We thought we'd put plans in place to keep it from happening, but we found out that some of the store owners were getting strong-armed."

"Strong-armed, how?" Kyle asked.

Landon answered him. "They were offered two, sometimes three times what their businesses were worth if they sold it after the renovations."

"I see," Symphony stated. "So, what now?'

"Now," Landon continued, "we add an amendment to the contracts that stipulate how long the store owners must own the business before selling, and that the only corporation they can sell to is Enrich Corp, as well as prohibiting large-scale luxury housing in the area. We want all housing to be affordable to middle-class residents."

"But what does all this mean for me and my business?" Symphony asked.

"We wanted you to be aware of some of the tactics developers are using to get into our neighborhood," Ethan stated.

Symphony saw Kyle straighten in his chair, look at her, and then back at Ethan and Landon. "Have any of the owners been harmed…physically?" Kyle asked.

Ethan and Landon looked at each other. It was Landon who finally spoke. "Yes."

Symphony looked at her husband and held his eyes. She knew he wanted to say something, but he was gauging her reaction to the news first.

"One of the store owners was approached by Cavanaugh Construction to buy her dry-cleaning business. She refused, and a week later her business was set on fire. The fire chief confirmed it was arson. She'd been sleeping upstairs and barely made it out alive. She's fine now, but it could have been really bad if the building hadn't been equipped with a sprinkler system."

"Again, what's the point, here? Wait..." She thought for a moment. "Cavanaugh Construction...Kenny Cavanaugh?"

They all turned to look at her.

"Yes," Landon stated. "Do you know him?"

"I met him on my last visit here. He was meeting with Terry at the same hotel where Ricco and I were staying." She paused. "Do you think he had something to do with the fire?" She thought about Ricco. Even though her friend denied it, she was sure Ricco was still stuck on the man.

"There was no evidence linking the company or any of his employees to the fire, but some of the business owners aren't convinced he wasn't involved," Ethan said. He looked at Kyle and Symphony before continuing. "Now, some of the owners are leery of anyone new. They want all business owners to also be residents of the neighborhood."

So that was it, she thought to herself. Symphony looked at Kyle, who had a slight frown on his face. "But we have no intentions to move here. I mean, I hadn't even planned on running the store myself."

"We know that, but I'm afraid you may be snubbed out if they don't feel like you're there for the benefit of the neighborhood."

They all talked for a while longer before they all went on a tour of the neighborhood. Both Ethan and Landon were pretty sure that with the new policies in place, the larger developers would not bother the current business owners any further.

Kyle was impressed with their ideas and was positive Symphony's would do well in the area. He was also in favor of buying a residence so they would have somewhere to stay when they came to check on the shop. They decided to set up a meeting for the following day to go over paperwork and plans to renovate the existing building.

When they returned to Phoenix Industries, Ethan wanted to show Kyle his new set of golf clubs.

Somehow on the tour, they'd started talking about golf, and Ethan found out Kyle was a golf instructor.

"Do you mind if I go speak to Terry?" she asked Kyle. "I want to know if he knows anything about Ricco and that Cavanaugh guy."

Kyle hesitated for only an instant, and she almost changed her mind. "Go ahead, baby. I'll meet you there."

"Are you sure?"

"I'm sure you love only me," he stated simply in her ear before placing a sweet kiss on her lips.

When she went to Terry's office, she noticed the secretary was not the same woman she'd seen in that position the last time she was there. This one was pleasant looking and quite pretty.

"May I help you?" she asked.

"I would like to see Mr. Phoenix, if he's not busy."

"Do you have an appointment?" she asked, knowing good and well she would know if he had an appointment or not.

"No, but since I was in the building, I thought I'd see if he was free." The woman had the nerve to run her eyes up and down Symphony, as if sizing her up. Symphony took back her "pleasant looking" assessment from earlier.

"Your name?" she finally asked.

"Symphony James…Dean. Sorry, just got married. Symphony Dean," she corrected herself.

The woman's mouth literally fell open when she gave her name. She recovered quickly, but Symphony wondered if maybe Terry had mentioned her to the woman.

She heard her on the phone saying, "Mr. Phoenix, Symphony Dean is here to see you."

Before the secretary had the phone back on the hook, Terry's door was opening.

"Symphony?" he asked, "What are you doing here?"

The secretary, Symphony noticed, had not returned to her work, but was instead looking on with interest. Symphony also noticed that Terry looked at the woman with an expression she couldn't quite place. Whatever it was, it gave her a weird vibe.

"Hello, Terry. I hope I'm not interrupting anything."

"No…no, come on in." He turned to his secretary. "Ava, you can go ahead to lunch now, if you want."

"But I thought…"

"If you don't mind," he cut her off, "bring me back my usual."

Symphony looked back at Terry's secretary and noticed she had not taken her eyes off her.

She stepped farther into the office, Terry closed the door and walked to his desk chair but didn't sit. Symphony wanted to ask him what that was all about.

"Your secretary was giving me the once over."

"Yeah, she's heard your name once or twice." Symphony cocked a brow at him. "Please, sit." He said, his hand out toward the chair in front of his desk. He sat too.

She really wanted to know what he'd said to his secretary about her, then she realized she didn't care. "I just stopped by to say hello. It would have been really rude of me to be in the building and not at least come and say hello."

"Ethan told me he was meeting with you today."

"Yes, he told me about the fire and Cavanaugh Construction."

"I don't believe for a minute that Kenny had anything to do with that."

"I was hoping you would say that."

"Ricco?"

"Yeah, what do you know?"

"I know he's pretending he's not thinking about her.

286

"She's doing the same."

They sat in an uncomfortable silence for a few beats. "I just wanted to make sure you're ok," Symphony finally said.

"I'm not going to lie, at first, I was really hurt. I'd bought that house hoping you'd be in it with me. That night in your hotel room when you told me that you were in love with Kyle, I just felt like all my plans for the future were dead. Later…much later, I realized I was in love with the idea of having a wife and a family." He frowned with an almost imperceptible shake of his head. "Don't get me wrong, Symphony, I did love you. I always will, but I love you enough to want you to be happy. I also love me enough to want to be happy." His eyes were serious. "Are you happy, Symphony?"

"Yes, Terry, I am. We both are."

"Well, then, I'm happy for you both."

The office door opened. Ava announced, "Mr. Phoenix, there's a Mr. Dean here."

"I thought you were going to lunch?" Terry asked, looking surprised to see her just burst into his office.

"I decided to wait for you."

Symphony stood when Kyle walked in. Ava had not moved. She stood there expectantly, staring at

Terry. Symphony and Kyle looked at each other and then toward Terry and Ava.

Ava let the door close with her still in the office. Terry walked around his desk and beckoned Ava to him.

"Kyle and Symphony Dean, this is Ava Fletcher," he hesitated only a moment before adding, "My girlfriend."

She smiled up at him, very pleased, before extending a hand to Symphony and Kyle.

"It's very nice to meet you," she said to Symphony and Kyle, sincerely. "I hear congratulations are in order."

"Thank you," The Deans said in unison. Symphony felt Kyle's arm slide around her waist.

"Yes, congratulations, to you both," Terry said, walking over to shake Kyle's hand.

"Thank you, Terry," Kyle said. "And thank you again for everything you and your family did in the rescue of Cadence and my parents. We will forever be in your debt."

Terry nodded. "I'm glad everything turned out ok, man."

"You ready to go, hun?" Kyle asked her.
Symphony nodded.

"We hope to see you two at dinner tonight. You will be joining us, won't you?" he asked Terry and Ava.

Terry's look of surprise told Symphony that he hadn't expected to go, or to even be asked to go.

"Sure, we'll be there," he said, and Ava looked up at him with a delighted grin.

Terry looked happy, and Symphony truly hoped he was. He was a good man and deserved to be as happy as she and her husband were.

Symphony and Kyle walked out of Terry's office. She looked up at the man she loved and wondered how she'd gotten so lucky.

"I sure do love you, Mr. Dean."

"I sure am glad, because you're stuck with me for life."

His words were music to her ears.

Dear Readers,

I hope you enjoyed Symphony's journey as much as I enjoyed writing her story for you. There were so many times over the past two years that I sat at the computer wanting to find out who Symphony would choose, but she took her precious time in sharing that knowledge with me. I hope you also enjoyed getting a glimpse of your favorite Phoenix men and their wives.

Thank you so much for your continued support and always wanting more. Maybe one day, we'll find out what's going on with Ricco and the gorgeous and mysterious Kenny Cavanaugh.

Joyful Reading,

Natasha Simmons

One Choice Away